On the Rocks

On the Rocks

A Novella

Theodora Bishop

Texas Review Press
Huntsville, Texas

Printed in the United States of America

FIRST EDITION
Requests for permission to acknowledge material from this work should be sent to:

Permissions
Texas Review Press
English Department
Sam Houston State University
Huntsville, TX 77341-2146

Cover design: Nancy Parsons
Author photo: Daniel Bishop

Library of Congress Cataloging-in-Publication Data

Names: Bishop, Theodora, 1989- author.
Title: On the rocks : a novella / Theodora Bishop.
Description: First edition. | Huntsville, Texas : Texas Review Press, [2018]
Identifiers: LCCN 2017055383 (print) | LCCN 2017057113 (ebook) | ISBN 9781680031539 (ebook) | ISBN 9781680031522 | ISBN 9781680031522¬(pbk.)
Subjects: LCSH: Mothers and daughters--Fiction. | Bereavement--Fiction. | Weddings--Fiction. | LCGFT: Domestic fiction. | Novellas.
Classification: LCC PS3602.I7656 (ebook) | LCC PS3602.I7656 O5 2018 (print) |
DDC 813/.6--dc23
LC record available at https://lccn.loc.gov/2017055383

To my parents, Lee and Eric

He would come down laughing over something fearfully funny he had been saying to a star, but he had already forgotten what it was, or he would come up with mermaid scales still sticking to him, and yet not be able to say for certain what had been happening.

— J.M. Barrie
Peter Pan

On the Rocks

Chapter One

It was springtime, almost a year after Sebastian died, when my mother phoned to tell me she was throwing a bridal shower for herself, and that I'd sure as dickens better be there: "You're the Maid of Honor, Eva. So no excuses, m'kay?"

My mother, Leonora Marino, was betrothed to the owner of a used car dealership called The Lemon Tree. One unfortunate detail about her fiancé's claim to fame being that its office and lots were painted bladder-stimulant yellow. This meant it was only natural that upon crossing into The Lemon Tree's domain, you became senseless, pervaded by a wild urge to pee. I often noticed potential customers swaying as they waited to be assisted, bouncing on their heels; their general conduct derived not from impatience, but rather from an effort to disguise their discomfort. But perhaps my mother's soon-to-be-hubby designed the space precisely so the hooey of swapping countless tons of metal for the big bucks was done swiftly.

Taking into account his bowed legs, his sideburns that collected floating air particles, Ted Turbine resembled one of those dopey Pekingese that impulse moves altruistic chumps to raise. I'll never be able to shake my first face-to-face encounter with Ted Turbine and that hairdo, a style that could easily have been clipped from the ass of a marmot and basted to his scalp. And despite my best efforts, I still haven't decided whether the guy's mutton chops were more redolent of a pedophile or Mr. Darcy. The semblance could swing either way.

Ted Turbine was roughly my mother's size and height, which meant slimmer than me and shorter, too—qualities I tried to think of as among his few assets, but which ultimately made me feel trollish. I am six-foot-two, what polite people insultingly describe as "big-boned," and had somehow managed to reject every one of my mother's ultra-feme genes. Even in baby pictures, it's clear I had inherited Dad's placemat of carob-brown hair and arched brows; the crooked mouth that gave passersby the impression that we were perpetually cringing.

Dad passed away five years ago, but when he was alive, one of his golfing friends said he was a dead ringer for Chevy Chase. Given Dad's custom of bearing about his vintage golf clubs with the same artlessness with which Thor wields his hammer, I sincerely hoped that Dad's pal owed his appraisal to *Caddyshack*. Once heard, I couldn't shake the comparison, and to this day I believe I can see traces of Chevy Chase in me—the Chevy Chase in *The National Lampoon* series—the unfailingly gung-ho, no matter how severely the universe is against him Chevy Chase. That was the oddity of Eva Marino that greeted me in the mirror.

Something important to consider is that though Ted Turbine glommed onto my mother ever since she agreed to go out with him, I was convinced my mother understood that, like Dad, whose entrepreneurial angst had drawn him to frequent travel, Ted Turbine's job took him places. There always seemed to be some new used car convention or scrap yard to mine—in addition to peddling used cars and attending cult-like gatherings dedicated to the art of luring desperate sods to his lot, Ted Turbine passed his hours scouting and assembling questionable scraps of automobile parts. It wasn't difficult for me to imagine him burrowing into some dump, sniffing out the best of the junk, only to return to his dealership, arms laden with riffraff.

All of which is to say that in the month leading up to the day Ted Turbine popped the question, I had the feeling my mother had already gleaned she could tolerate her new beau for the long haul because he would often be gone. The imminent date for their wedding had been decided as speedily as Ted Turbine proposed and my mother agreed. Like she had some life-threatening malady and needed to accelerate things, she leapt from point A to point B.

Never mind that things were fine before Ted Turbine stepped into the frame, and Ted Turbine's offer became the point C that my mother was desperate to reach.

We were sitting at The Grumpy Monk Tavern, a sea of depleted Mai Tais between us when—leaning forward, her mouth a slash of coral lipstick—Leonora Marino professed her hope that "Teddy rides away as often as he rides me!"

I doubt my mother has any recollection of ever having declared as much. What was said at The Grumpy Monk not only stayed at The Grumpy Monk, but was often forgotten by whoever had said it.

That Ted Turbine was conveniently away in the weeks leading up to the wedding also meant there was no Ted Turbine to worry about when it came to preparing for the big day or my mother's bridal shower, either. Who cares if only a handful of guests would be attending the wedding? My mother declared the two weeks leading up to the day she agreed to have and to hold, "Love in the Time of Haul-Ass Marino." Having already forgotten, I suppose, that she would soon shed the "Marino," only to take the surname of a turbomachine.

To be fair, even when Dad was there, I don't think my mother ever fully settled into being a Marino. The name didn't suit her any better than it did me. Where "Leonora Marino" called to mind a humpbacked old woman—one most likely wearing a babushka in the witchy bravura of Baba Yaga—"Eva Marino" sounded like a brand of gnocchi to me.

I suspected Ted Turbine wasn't all that deflated when his schedule enabled him to miss out on my mother's endeavors to wrangle citronella-scented tiki torches out of old wine bottles. Lately, all my mother could talk about were starfish centerpieces and fishing net garlands—the latter to be embellished with driftwood peanuts. Time-consuming D.I.Y. décor whose conception I blamed on Pinterest.

Prior to his latest departure, Ted Turbine deposited a substantial sum into my mother's account, giving her buttocks an equally generous squeeze. I'd seen the whole outrage occur, and yes, the sight was as disturbing as it sounds.

But for now, Ted Turbine was down in Texas, participating in some snooze-fest about selling used fuel pumps. And because I've spent the majority of my life in the highbrow hamlet of Ship Bottom, New Jersey—for which somewhere there must exist an ordinance that every house and shopfront boast an ebullient shade of sherbet and some form of nautical lawn ornament—Texas seemed like its own planet. For instance, I think "Texas," and imagine endless flat ranches and stirrups and men's dress shirts embroidered with roses. Sweet tea and smoked brisket, swaths of armadillos splayed in ludicrous positions across the asphalt.

"Is it true that everything's bigger in Texas?" I'd made a crack at Ted Turbine, who ran his hand through his chia pet mop, gazed down at his saddle shoes, and said to me, in earnest, "Let me check on that."

In any case, I didn't have a problem with my mother's fiancé per se; I had a problem with the fact that Ted Turbine thought festooning his lot with inflatable air dancers was okay. For yet another disquieting feature of The Lemon Tree was that it was the only business in a fifty-mile radius that perverted its property with those things, which you could see clear from the turnpike, wiggling in the breeze like tubular creeps. That Ted Turbine believed that rainbow of air dancers was an effective way to bait customers did not sit well with me: "If you want to sell people's smelly old cars," I told him, "you're going to have to get rid of those things."

But like any guy who was crazy enough about my mother to not only ask her to marry him, but to understand that her twenty-eight-year-old daughter was also part of the package, Ted Turbine only patted me delicately on the shoulder, like he was afraid of knocking me over. Apparently, he thought I was kidding, which was delightfully odd of him. Up until then, similar incidences had me convinced Ted Turbine didn't have an ironic bone in his body, which probably explains how he could endure me and my mother. Anyone else would've thought Ted Turbine was after her money, but to those who actually knew my mother—i.e., her daughter—it was obvious that given the track of her spending, there was no way Leonora Marino could last on what remained of Dad's savings. Besides, despite his obscene troupe of air dancers, Ted Turbine already had a name for himself. So maybe his investment in sacks of oscillating fabric wasn't strong enough to kill his position.

But what I'm trying to talk about has less to do with Ted Turbine than what my mother's decision to marry him meant for us as mother and daughter. What I am trying to talk about is the death of my best friend Sebastian, and how it changed everything.

Chapter Two

I'd grown up with Sebastian, best friend and lover—both names I'd called our neighbor when I was ten-years-old. I was too young, my mother had laughed, to know anything about what the latter meant.

What my mother didn't get was that Sebastian was also the first boy who'd touched me. And when I say "touch," I don't mean in a figurative sense. Though I suppose both the literal and figurative meanings of the word hold true.

And so to cope with Sebastian's death, a tragedy that continues to teach me how differently humans grieved, my mother cut off her hair and let it go gray. Before she laid her Facebook account to rest, she posted pictures of all the clothing from Chico's and J. Crew she'd amassed, and volunteered them to any takers who fit a size 6. And if that wasn't drastic enough, she resigned from her book club. Her wardrobe now consisted of peasant tops and maxi skirts with botanical patterns. Also, wide-legged rompers that gave her the appearance of an overgrown toddler.

The real cherry happened when I told my mother I was taking a leave of absence that winter, and she thought I was pregnant: "I'm going to be a Baba!" she'd cooed.

Unless Ship Bottom was on the cusp of its first miracle, such a reality could not have been possible.

Watching my mother's face light up before telling her my news, I was almost tempted to sustain the charade. Stuff a pillow under my sweatshirt and feign morning sickness in the hopes my mother would come to my aid.

Naturally, there was no need. Because together, Leonora Marino and I were an inexorable force. Plus, my mother was in no mind to lessen the time we spent together. In fact, though I sometimes wanted her to give me space, leave me to hibernate in the fort of pillows and blankets I'd made in front of my TV, it ultimately did not matter how exasperating she could be. Though she was the one approaching the threshold of her second marriage, I needed her more than ever.

And so when I broke down and explained the real reason for my leave-taking—that I was depressed and could barely get out of bed—my mother insisted I see someone, then suggested we order takeout from Magic Noodle House: "You love their pot stickers, don't you, Eva?"

After my first appointment with Shiloh, my mother rushed over to my apartment, demanding to know how my session went: "Are you feeling better yet?"

How she thought one session with Shiloh flicked some switch on inside me and made me suddenly happy, was beyond me. But then I can remember how I'd watched her scramble out of her car, completely disheveled and looking like hell to see how I was. She was wearing a gray tracksuit, and her hair was balled about the crown of her head with a scarf. The oatmeal-colored fabric strained at her forehead and gave the impression of her having had a recent injection. At the time, I'd had to consciously shut down my mind to stop myself from crying. What I didn't think my mother understood was that her writing off Ted Turbine's earnings in service of my counseling translated into my spending an hour each week in Shiloh's luxurious office, seething in silent rage.

It took months before Shiloh got me to talk. I offered about as much as a mute: eye contact, a couple of head nods.

And so when we first started out, Shiloh suggested I try a Buddha Board, on which I was supposed to channel my thoughts through a water-soaked brush.

The Buddha Board didn't make me feel very Zen-like, however. I mean, I couldn't think of anything significant to write on it, so I'd end up drawing stick figures and scribbling "Namaste" in the corner. The only feel-good part of the process was that the board erased itself, which was the whole magic and meaning behind it. Was watching the worries I'd painted magically dissolve an illustration in reverse of what Shiloh wanted me to do—to let go? That I didn't have to bother scrubbing the board and could just put the thing away when I was done was cool. That is, until one day when I was feeling reasonably creative and didn't even get the chance to appreciate the frog prince I'd drawn before it hopped right off the page.

Given that the mandala art practiced by monks seemed fairly related to the Buddha Board ritual, I didn't expect the Buddha Board and I were destined to be besties. After all, I'd seen a real sand mandala demonstration once upon a field trip for a Religious Studies class I was taking at Skidmore.

I have to admit that I probably should have reviewed the readings my professor assigned before tagging along on the voyage to that monastery in the mountains of holiness what's-it. I wasn't prepared for what Professor Gutman called the "pièce de résistance." Apparently, this didn't consist of a scoop of gelato plopped atop one of those oozing fudge cakes you order at Chili's. In the language of Professor Gutman, the "pièce de résistance" referred to the part where the monks destroy the very thing they'd spent weeks toiling away at. But who knows how long those monks with their bald heads and cumbersome robes spent huddled together, creating that beautiful sand painting?

Luckily, I didn't blurt, "STOP!"—which was what I had been thinking, among other one-syllable words—when I witnessed the monks ruining their art. As I would later learn, the whole impetus behind their dumping that colorful sand into the brook was to demonstrate that nothing is permanent, but if Professor Gutman wanted to teach us about the life cycle, we shouldn't have had to travel all that way to learn from a bunch of celibates with donuts for hairlines. My classmates and I could have just screened the scene in *The Lion King* where Mufasa kicks the bucket and had a good cry. To behold them chanting with the gravity of pubescent choirboys belting the opening measures of "All Creatures of Our God and King" over the artwork they were ravaging didn't seem healthy to me. And that brings me in a roundabout, mandala-like way, to the Buddha Board and the deficiency of progress in terms of my pursuit for wellness. Because I didn't like thinking about life as this journey where someone pressed "play" at the start of your birth, and then "eject" whenever he or she itched. I found it more healing to pull on my *I Love Lucy* pajamas and burrow under the covers. When you lost a loved one, it didn't seem fair that the world still expected you to keep going. My mother and I had already lost my father five years before Sebastian drowned off the coast of Ship Bottom.

And then one day, my Buddha Board trial a flop, I opened up to Shiloh after she asked me about Sebastian: "Your mother mentioned him?"

"My mother?" I shouted, incensed. What was Leonora Marino doing, putting her hands into my—

And then I understood. My mother was coming in to see Shiloh, too.

It was during that session I explained how half the time I could barely breathe and how it was akin to negotiating a roomful of racing bats that flapped in your face, smothering you. That's the way I described it to Shiloh. The rest of the time, I told her, I had to stop whatever I was doing and arrange myself into corpse pose.

Basically, the nuts and bolts of Shiloh's response was confirmation that this was a problem. Then she recommended I start a gratitude journal to find an outlet to deal with my anger.

"Physical activity would also be good for you."

"Are you calling me fat?" I fired back.

"Of course not," Shiloh shook her princess head.

I was so used to spending every moment I wasn't on my own with Leonora Marino, I'd forgotten what it was like to be around other people not familiar with our sense of humor.

From the beginning, Shiloh seemed to buy into my looking for scapegoats to pin down my grief, a state of mind I likened to walking through cobwebs. Finding my way out of whatever lingual pattern I'd begun the second I opened my mouth was like pulling myself up a ladder made of pudding, the rungs kept slipping. Ultimately, it didn't matter how little sense I was making. Shiloh always wore an expression so perfectly calm and fixed, you'd think she were one of those storybook princesses who communed with animals and plants. What I mean is that it was good for me to get out of my apartment and sit in that woman's office. Even though perching on Shiloh's fancy leather couch meant sweating my ass off as I heard myself talk, I pushed myself to keep going, no matter the cyclical thoughts. And as winter thawed into spring, I decided Shiloh earned every penny when she was with me. I was grateful to my mother for insisting I go. I was grateful to Ted Turbine, too. Without that fool, there's no way I would have been able to finagle Shiloh's rates. Apparently, the health insurance for a magazine columnist didn't cover therapy for employees at the end of their wits.

And so I didn't forget it was thanks to Ted Turbine, whose wallet my mother had no problem accessing, that my sessions with Shiloh were covered.

And my mother's sessions too, I knew.

It was under Shiloh's counsel that spring—the spring of my mother's wedding, the one that nipped at the heels of the spring we lost Sebastian—that I began attempting to iron out my angst at Fountain-of-You Yoga. And no sooner had my mother caught me toting my mat on Bearded Clam Avenue than she piggybacked on my new practice. Defining the common denominator of our lived experience as our efforts to "forgive and forget," and our memberships at Fountain-of-You Yoga as a means to do that.

"We can reach nirvana together!" she squealed, seizing my hands in hers. The earnestness with which she clung resolute as one proposing we conduct our oath in blood. "You and me, downward-dogging our ways back to happiness! What do you say?"

I wondered if Shiloh had encouraged my mother to go to Fountain-of-You, too, or if the whim was my mother's alone. Did it even make sense for Shiloh to treat my mother and me both? At times, I'd look at Leonora Marino and think: *we are the same person*. But for the most part, I'd baulk at the things my mother would say, the things I'd been catching her do, since I was a little girl running feral about Ship Bottom with our neighbor Sebastian.

At any rate, I told my mother I'd be happy to have her tag along to yoga with me: "Of course, I want to spend each week in Warrior I and II with you. Heck, I'm ready to arc into cow pose."

Which is how Thursday nights that spring meant tree posing on a sweaty mat beside my mother, followed by a date at The Grumpy Monk Tavern. Seeing as my mother and I were still in mourning, the weekly catharsis of cocktails and adrenaline was a godsend.

But let me start from the beginning.

My mother and I have always subsisted as two very different sides of the same coin. Forget that she had several decades on me. While I had already encountered vastly different experiences than my mother, she and I were both stubborn and interminably young at heart. All of which is to say that I knew my mother's second marriage couldn't last if her husband-to-be's expectations of her were normal. That is, if Ted Turbine expected her to be faithful.

Before she started joining me for yoga, I'd prepared to blame my unraveling life on my mother and her theory of love: that carefree lifestyle she seemed to think of as seamless, but through which I saw only large, gaping holes.

Now I have no intention of blatantly attributing the new life phases my mother and I began on the death of my best friend, but if you follow the breadcrumbs, I believe the spring Sebastian drowned dramatically altered our paths.

Now, I wasn't at the point where I considered Sebastian an angel or anything. I'm not a squat into religion. The few times I went to church, I felt like a gherkin crammed into an airtight jar of kosher dills. Even so, I needed to find something to believe in and wondered if desperation was the secret to faith, or at least what pushed those who believed in nothing toward something. Because I eventually decided I could believe in Sebastian somehow guiding my mother and me, if that's what it took to get me out of bed in the morning.

But even when I kept digging myself deeper, I suppose you could say I felt Sebastian with me. Because once I put stock into the idea that Sebastian was somehow watching over us, it made sense that he was in many ways linked to my mother's and my transformed outlooks. Sebastian had always seemed too good for the world.

But then I'm biased, of course. Because I had been in love with Sebastian since we were kids.

Chapter Three

It was hard to believe that the wedding was just two weeks away. Even harder to stomach was the fact that my mother wanted to host a weekend-long bridal shower in the first place. Roping me in as Maid of Honor only served as further proof that my mother and I had no friends. I must have realized that before my mother even told me she was tying the knot again. That, for all intents and purposes, all my mother and I had left was each other.

If we were to divide the Marino side into categories, our relatives would fall into either the vaguely awful or the certifiably horrible, which explained the necessity to avoid them entirely. Dad's eldest sister Josey fell into the latter category.

After all, the impetus behind the melodramatic bon voyage Facebook status my mother published before putting her Facebook to bed was owed to her sister-in-law's onslaught of comments, the offensive links and YouTube videos she posted. As if that wasn't bad enough, there existed an entire private thread in which Aunt Josey enumerated my mother's offenses. Often underscoring her allegations by calling my mother "tart," among other names perhaps more commonly fired off in the BBC costume dramas my aunt was known to watch. These insults seemed even more disturbing coming from Aunt Josey, who one Easter showed up wearing a t-shirt depicting *The Passion*, the goriness of which would give the chest-bursting scene in *Alien* a run for its money.

So when it came to conceiving a guest list for her shower, I imagined my mother must have been grasping for straws. Ultimately, she made a wise move by inviting a handful from her side of the family. The tolerable and strangely likeable members of the Kaminskis.

The accepted invitees included my uncle Tuck and aunt Ginny, their daughter, Vivian, and Vivian's six-year-old, Charlize, whose precociousness frightened me. My mother was so desperate she even extended the call to Great Aunt Ethel, whose blood ties to our family I'd never fully gotten the hang of. My great aunt was a mystery to all ill-starred enough to encounter her. And because for all I know, she could be a century old, in my head she endures as "Mythic Ethel."

With the guest list confirmed, my mother decided to devise some sort of hashtag to label the hullaballoo. "What better way to commemorate my first-ever bridal party, if not with a hashtag? It's basically giving me permission to ring my wedding bells into the ether. Don't you think, Eva?"

Despite the social media-driven animosity from the Marinos and her subsequent severance from Facebook, what my mother couldn't give up was her Twitter account. We'd be leaving Fountain-of-You Yoga, having withstood a long-ass sequence of pigeon pose, when I would realize I was walking along, talking to no one. Only to turn and find my mother stopped in the middle of the sidewalk, fingertips jitterbugging her Android, her face illuminated like a terrific moon. If the world was all a stage and we its players, then in my mother's theatre, her script was written for Twitter.

The bridal party hashtags she came up with, but ultimately decided to trash—"None of them are good enough, Eva!"—were as follows:

#WhenLifeGivesULemons
#TurbinoSquared
#LeonoraIsGettingMarriedMoFos!

In the days leading up to the shower, I offered to take my mother to David's Bridal. Though the wedding was going to be a small ceremony, I assumed my mother would want to wear something special. She was, on every other account, going all out.

But the blowback of my stomaching the surprise of my mother's impending marriage, all the while trying to be a good daughter, came when my mother shot me a pained look. Insisting that the selection offered at Consignment Castle was more along the lines of the type of dress she was after.

To give Leonora Marino's preference some context, my tried and true Yoda tree topper was the only object I'd found worth nabbing from Consignment Castle, and that was years back. Back before we lost Dad and I felt my world start to turn, only to eventually plummet, depositing me face-down in a rut after we lost Sebastian.

I'll admit that though The Grand Master smelled like old socks, my Yoda tree topper was well worth the purchase; that he croaked, "Merry the force, you shall have," when his motion detector sporadically kicked in, was reason enough. But a wedding dress from Consignment Castle belonged in a class all to itself. The very idea made me think of lipstick stains, cheap champagne, and honeymoon suites with congested Jacuzzis.

"I'm a hipster," my mother insisted as she charged determinedly into the racks at Consignment Castle, a caballero in service to a damsel trapped among stratums of secondhand material.

"I don't get it," I protested. Having already dissuaded her against her first pick: a fit and flare dress whose greasy train gave my mother the appearance of trailing a trash bag. "You used to say wearing strangers' clothes gave you the willies, that it was like wearing their skin. What happened to that?"

Pausing just slightly, my mother opted to interpret my question rhetorically and carry on through the rows of used clothing.

Three hours later, the ball gown she settled on was marked by chutes of taffeta whose bouncy gradation made me think of cake frosting. Its bodice was also odorous of antiperspirant.

The contrast between the aesthetics my mother went for in her wedding with Dad, and her forthcoming one with Ted, could not have been starker. In what I imagine to be a burst of feminist energy, before she wed a Marino, the freshly engaged Leonora Kaminski chose a colored pantsuit over the customary white dress. Actually, when it came to planning their wedding, I can easily imagine my mother tipping her head back and laughing, "What planning?" had anyone asked about the progress she was making. For in a gesture to cut herself further off from her parents, my mother confessed to having been intent on having a practical ceremony—no bells and whistles, only witnesses and the officiant she described as having "a curdled complexion" were in attendance. And as if to remind her that for twenty-three years she and that man in the picture shared a life together, my mother continued to keep the one photo from the service displayed on the mantel.

Rather than a romantic gazebo or a sensible altar, the sage face of a soon-to-be risen Jesus gazing fondly down at their union, the mottled aqua tiles of a courthouse basement served as my parents' wedding day backdrop. In the photo, my mother sports a tangerine-colored pantsuit, an enormous corsage blooming on her wrist, while Dad looks like a downright seadog, decked in white and navy. The photo resonates high school homecoming, my parents posing awkwardly, their expressions trapped in some bizarre phase between glower and grin. As if my parents were jointly averse to echoing a zealous photographer's hackneyed variety of, "Say cheese!"

"Say, Havarti!" or, "Say, Camembert, you lovebirds!"

Lovebirds my foot.

If you were oblivious to the circumstances behind the photo, you'd reason my folks were estranged cousins posing in an asbestos-ridden YMCA. But then estranged cousins wasn't so far from how I ultimately came to understand their relationship to be.

Chapter Four

The evenings we spent at The Grumpy Monk Tavern when my harried mother spouted some outlandish concern or other were nothing compared to her onslaught of midnight phone calls eliciting my counsel.

In the weeks since she agreed to "until death do us part" with the used car dealer, my mother's subjects ranged from cake flavors—"I told Cynthia Marsh I'm aiming for something tropical, so now we've narrowed it down to passion fruit, rum, and banana!"—to guest favors—"Monogrammed flip flops or raffia fans? Tell me quick, Eva. I'll go with whatever your gut says!"

I'd done virtually nothing in terms of aiding my mother's planning, save try to calm her. Perusing a copy of *Bride-to-Be Magazine* in the dentist office waiting room the day after my mother selected her wedding dress filled me with dread. Between its wedding personality quizzes and charts of dresses organized by body type, the material seemed more discouraging than helpful. Paging through spread after spread of models who looked fresh out of high school depressed me. I had let myself go over the winter—I was like a bear still in hibernation: somnolent and hairy, all I needed was a pot of honey. Come spring, it had gotten to the point that I wasn't sure if I could brush my hair without breaking my comb. Basically, no sooner did I let myself loose about Ship Bottom then I hulked about town, distrustful of passersby, wondering what the hell was that awful smell. It took longer than I care to admit before I realized I was the one that stunk. To top it off, I'd even gotten into the habit of wearing my sunglasses so often, it must have been months since I cleaned them when the cashier at Wawa asked if I needed a tissue: "Ma'am, did you get shat on?"

"Since when did I graduate from 'Miss' to 'Ma'am?'" I shouted at him. Storming out of Wawa with my Banana Cream Smoothie and trying to channel the mantras of Shiloh: *Within me is a peace that cannot be disturbed.* Or was it, *Within me is a peace that wants to throw its digitus manus up at the world?*

It was really too bad my go-to intonation ended up being the Disney song that I believed was destined to be the death of me. If I heard Queen Elsa belt, "Let it go!" one more time, I thought I'd be the one with the power to make ice.

Breathe, Eva, Breathe. I'd count down from ten before I turned my Honda on and gingerly buckled myself in.

After the dental hygienist called me in, I was thinking so hard about my mother's impending nuptials and trying not to nip my hygienist's fingers while her hands were stuffed in my mouth, that I lost track of myself. By the time my appointment was over and Dr. Patel had brandished my x-rays and cheerfully informed me of the impacted wisdom tooth that needed prompt removal, I was prepared to blame this news on my preoccupation with my mother's marriage. I would have to have what little wisdom I had left extracted, literally.

I had been pondering such thoughts and thus tuning Dr. Patel out when he and the hygienist resumed prodding around in my mouth, exchanging technical terms and nodding with conviction.

Let it go, I told myself. When really, I could have punched a hole in the wall.

In the meantime, there occurred a much-welcomed, if not disconcerting lull in my mother's deluge of calls. For two days, my mother did not phone. The morning of day three of her silence, however, she made up for her quiet. I woke to six missed calls, two voicemails, and a text on my cell:

Don't tell me you're joining the league of daughters who disown their mothers. CALL ME NOW!

She picked up on the first ring. Her voice was high, pitchy—I could tell she'd been drinking.

My mother wanted me to come over immediately for an emergency rendezvous at her place.

"You can help me finish this pitcher of margaritas!" she told me. "Limes were on sale at Sam's Club, but what does one do with ten pounds of limes? So, here I am. Drinking allll byyyy myyyyselffff."

It was too easy to picture my mother conducting an invisible orchestra as she slurred along to Eric Carmen.

"Mom, it's eight o'clock in the morning."

"Right you are, kiddo. See—aren't you glad Dad and I sent you to Moore Hedge Academy? Smart as a whip, that you are!"

A fan of *Downton Abbey*, my mother sometimes slipped into parroting the syntax of a particular class of post-Edwardian Yorkshire accent. I could detect neither reason nor warning before she did this. Sober or plastered, my mother was prone to randomly falling in step with the Ladies of Grantham.

I could hear the roar of the blender from her end of the line. My mother snickering into the phone: "Eva, what is the reason for this dullness? Listen, daughter, are you coming or not?"

"I think you should move back home," my mother slurred the moment she winged open the door, her Shih Tzu Caboodle wheezing at her heels.

All I could do was remind her I was twenty-eight-years-old, and far past the age when living with one's able-bodied mother in the house one grew up in was acceptable.

"This isn't a conversation for the stoop." My mother pulled me into the hall, already clambering on. "We can redecorate, don't worry!" she shouted over her shoulder, her nylon peignoir billowing behind her as she rambled the stairwell. Leaving Caboodle to tilt his fluffy white head at me, sniff, then hightail it for the back door.

Whose idea had it been to fill a teenage girl's room with frills? I wondered, in awe of what I saw, having followed my mother up the stairs and down the hall. It had been years since I'd been in my old room.

It was like everything cloth vomited more cloth; I couldn't believe I used to like this stuff. And you couldn't escape the sheer pervasion of pink: crossing the threshold into my bedroom was like passing through an intestine, if intestines resembled the plastic models Sister Thomasina of Moore Hedge Academy used to demonstrate the digestive tract in Honors Anatomy.

The thought occurred to me, unbidden: *I'm going to die in here, aren't I?*

"Mom . . ."

"I know. I can get rid of them."

"Rid of—"

And then I saw them. The exemplary members of my mother's doll collection. All dozen or so populating the very armchair on which I had once consumed a summer reading's list worth of tragedies: *Crime and Punishment, Native Son*, *In Cold Blood*, and the comparatively chipper *Memoirs of a Geisha*. Like Moore Hedge Academy wanted its pupils to kill themselves.

My mother showed me where she thought we could put a futon and TV, thereby avoiding any unnecessary interruptions to my Netflix binge: "See, if we haul your old bed out and bring in one of those sleek Ikea numbers . . ."

Her plans for my childhood room went on, the arms of my mother's peignoir fanning as she pointed from this corner to that, wanding her margarita glass in the dramatic manner of a scepter. We could repaint and re-carpet, hang new curtains that did not look like something that belonged in *Anne of Green Gables*.

I stared at my mother's dolls, which ranged from the bloated-faced Cabbage Patch to your everyday Victorian mourning companion. My mother had even acquired a Barak Obama and a Sarah Palin Barbie, the additions of which were made more bizarre by the fact that my mother obviously had no interest in politics. Having subscribed her to *The New York Times* one year for Christmas, I'd come over not a week into the new year to find her pitching the front page into the fireplace.

"Kindling," she answered my blank expression, balling up the Arts section. "For Krishna. Now why don't you sign me up for that magazine you write for?"

Before I caved and gave my mother a gift subscription to *Eat Right!*, I had already been dreading her reaction to the content we published. I'd known the day would come that my mother would ask to read it. Though I'd scored an entry level job at *Eat Right!* fresh out of college—I was fortunate that at the time my boss, Olive, was scouring Ship Bottom for "Youth!" and "Fresh blood!"—I hadn't told my mother much about it. Given how when I wasn't toying around at my standing desk, I was changing the backdrop to my computer or fetching everyone else coffee, there wasn't much to say about my first months at *Eat Right!* In fact, the only responsibility required of me was preparing Olive's special "Volcanic Brew" coffee, which she took with a splash of kefir and a teaspoon of blackstrap molasses. A concoction I could not help but blame for the appalling deposits that everyone knew devastated the second-floor bathroom at half-past eleven. And so, having already worked several years for the same magazine, I was naturally caught off guard when my mother suddenly wanted to know everything my job at *Eat Right!* involved.

I wasn't surprised that she was more befuddled by the stuff we published than inspired to try some of the wellness recommendations herself. Since this was before my mother went on her juicing kick and got addicted to sharing pictures of everything she consumed on Twitter, I couldn't exactly imagine the woman who at that point sustained herself on Heath bars and cubed cheese preparing breakfast jars of self-rising chia seeds. But after I subscribed her, what surprised me was that from the first issue she received onward, my mother read every *Eat Right!* cover to cover.

But forget the pink and the frills and please don't think about the dolls. By the time I left my mother's, having joined her for a fresh batch of margaritas and a bag of stale Tostitos, she had managed to convince me to submit my two-week notice to my landlady.

Chapter Five

Growing up in the Marino family bungalow was like being raised a princess inside a life-sized sandcastle. The bungalow was constructed of adobe, calling to mind that ancient silt and dung blend made popular in the assemblage of pueblos. The fact that there was a dumbwaiter in our pantry further amplified the bungalow's grandiosity. Dumbwaiters were for people for whom it was necessary their cheese Danish and morning paper be conveyed via an elevator the size of a shoebox, and thus designated specifically for that purpose. Except, neither my Dad nor my mother had any use for the dumbwaiter, which my mother described as "touchingly bourgeoisie."

Before the decades of sea breezes turned it the color of a bad avocado, our bungalow bore the happy promise of a mint julep.

The best part was that Sebastian and his father Finn lived in a stumpy cottage down the block from it. What was so unusual about their cottage was that it was beige in a neighborhood where all the houses loomed in various shades of sorbet. And because Finn and Sebastian were only a stone's throw away, it seemed only natural that in the winters, when Dad went away on his clock-making expeditions, my mother decided we might as well make an impromptu jaunt down the beach to their place and say, "Hey, what's up?"

I hadn't thought much about how Dad fit into the picture when I was a kid. What difference did it make that my mother laughed harder and more often around Finn than she ever did around Dad? While Dad travelled the country peddling handmade cuckoo clocks like an artisanal pauper stuck in some fairy tale realm, it only seemed fair that my mother and I entertained ourselves in his absence. And so during the winters, we spent just as much time at our neighbors' cottage as we did in our bungalow. Wasn't there some saying to the effect, "Why walk when you can dance?"

After showing up unannounced on their doorstep became routine, Finn and Sebastian also began appearing at our place during the spells Dad was away. During that time, I came to think of my mother and me as belonging in an altered rendition of *Little Women.* My mother, flighty Jo, and me, sensible Beth, both under the influence of fictions Jo invented to entertain them while the man of the house was away.

After his father passed, Dad inherited a chain of four small motels along the coast. My grandfather coined the motels The Sea Grass Cove, The Mystic Mermaid, The Sanguine Seahorse, and The Pugnacious Pirate, drawing on the atmosphere of Ship Bottom—a blend of ice cream parlors, fitness clubs, aquatic-themed miniature golf courses, and boutiques whose offerings ranged from overpriced sand buckets to exfoliating scrubs, the sea salt of which was purportedly mined from the dank walls of Ship Bottom grottos.

As my parents and I occupied one of Ship Bottom's ginormous bungalows with the best ocean views, we were not only a spit's distance from Finn and Sebastian's, but also from The Sea Grass Cove.

Sure, the quartet of Marino motels were cornily named, but the motels themselves were quaint in a Mother Goose sort of way. There were the artificial palm trees and bamboo shoots shrouding The Sea Grass Cove property. The Pugnacious Pirate's neon-lit sign, shaped like a treasure trove which hung slightly askew—its swell of blinking jewels and doubloons joining the sequence of neon writing that characterized the shopfronts on the Seas-the-Day-Street in the summertime.

Once the motels passed to Dad, it was all goodbye, taxidermy sea gulls and shag rugs. Adios, barnacle-printed davenports and lampshades tasseled in dehydrated sea stars. Leonora Marino immediately took charge of revamping the Bates aesthetic of the guestrooms in which my grandfather had left them. Even the wood panel walls—suggestive of some beach bum's butchered body having been boarded inside of—were replaced with drywall painted with forests of coral and kelp. Her stint volunteering at the local children's library notwithstanding, I had never before seen my mother so invested in anything. It was not uncommon for Leonora Marino to dive headfirst into a project; what *was* unusual was for her to stick with it.

Dad was fifty-five when he died, and because I'd been the one to light the two numeral-shaped candles for the cake on the last birthday he was able to celebrate, his age is stamped as two wax "5's" in my mind. He had been growing pink in the face even before the awful summer Finn and Sebastian moved away, leaving me to pack up my things and be shipped off to Moore Hedge Academy.

Like most kids, I didn't think anything bad would ever happen to my family. Bad things happened to other families, not the Marinos. Innocent to the possibility that our lives could ever be touched by sorrow, I never would have imagined anything would come out of Dad being precipitously pink in the face, which to me seemed more like an attribute reminiscent of Santa Claus than a symptom to be wary of.

To this day, I feel terrible for ascribing Dad's ruddy color to his eating so much lobster—my mother was on smart terms with the Ship Bottom fishmonger, and so we did consume a good deal of lobster. But like so many of the yarns we spin as children, now that I have been given some perspective, I would do anything to take back what I said.

What I am trying to say is that it was only the start of life pulling the carpet out from under me and my mother. That Dad's raspberry complexion was in fact a sign of his health going sour, which may or may not have had to do with his consumption of lobster.

It has been five years since Dad's heart attack. Five years interposed with my mother wearing gaudy black outfits while she tried to keep Dad's motel business afloat at the same time she remade herself.

It has also been five years of me longing after Sebastian, who, even in his death, I continued to pine for.

But Sebastian's body was found in the spring.

Even now, I still must remind myself, repeat the fact aloud again and again until I can almost believe it.

Sebastian was found in the spring.

Sebastian was found last *spring.*

Up until Dad, nobody I'd closely known had ever passed. I was only a baby when my grandfather left. "Left" being a term my Dad preferred to use when it came to referring to what happened to my grandfather. "Left" seemed much more indicative of a story—a page you could mark and return to.

"Death," on the other hand, seemed more like an end stop. The point from which there is only one way to turn, and that's backwards.

In my favorite photo of my grandfather and me, he is holding the toddler version of me outside The Mystic Mermaid. The sun must have been shining harshly into our faces the day the photo was taken. Either that, or my grandfather and I were downright pissed—dressed in the bonnet and bloomers that characterized the garb of my childhood, I look especially incensed.

There are other pictures of us, of course, but it is from this one that I feel a special kinship between us.

Because my mother's maiden name was Kaminski, she had seen to hiring as many Polish immigrants as she could. It was, she told Dad, the least they could do.

It shames me to think that it was once normal to wake on a Saturday morning to Daria picking up my damp swimsuits and balled-up socks while Marek groomed our lawn when residents of Ship Bottom were still lounging in their pima cotton pajamas.

But with the Polish staff who cleaned The Sea Grass Cove

swinging by to tidy our rooms, the bungalow could feel like a top-notch resort. Owing to the cross-pollination of business and home, sometimes our bedding and towels got mixed up with those from the motel. I could always tell when the laundry had been swapped. Sometimes, I climbed into sheets bearing a seahorse insignia, for which I wondered with pleasure what guest would be sleeping in sheets monogrammed with my initials.

Yet as a kid, all the fuss for the sake of our bungalow was just par for the course. And I'd enjoyed getting in with the cleaning staff. My favorite maid Justina let me do all the stuff I wasn't normally allowed to when my mother asked her to be a doll and watch me for an hour or two. In the forgotten fitness center of our basement, Justina let me try out the treadmill, whose accidents involving cords getting wrapped around toddlers' necks had traumatized my mother. How the treadmill and rack of fitness balls ended up at my parents' in the first place are just another among the Marino clan's unsolvable mysteries. In a certain light, the equipment cast shadows of devices designed for torture, which was perhaps why Dad and my mother never opted to use them. In hindsight, I wish Dad had used them. Also, that he had forgone renting a golf cart and hiring a caddy every time he met his buddies at the country club. Maybe if he had taken better care of himself, not cared so much about the popularity of the motels, or travelled in the hopes of sharing the cuckoo clocks he made tediously by hand with the greater East Coast, he would still be around.

During the spells my mother entrusted Justina with watching me, Justina sometimes fried up batches of succulent apple dumplings and let me have as much ice cream on top as I wanted. The only problem was that whenever I indulged in those dumplings, I bewitched Justina with my gastrointestinal fits. Though I basically turned into Nosferatu after scarfing her dairy-smothered confections, my mother later consoled me by saying poor Justina probably endured far worse from the country she came from: "Our people come from a long line of suffering," my mother told me. Being the authority on Polish history, Leonora Marino had explained this to me on the same day she cleaned out Marvin and Gully's grocery of their kielbasa and cabbage.

I didn't pin down the sad truth of my digestive tract until my first semester at Moore Hedge Academy, when having polished off a bowl of cream of broccoli at the annual soup social, I helicoptered my hedge mates on my race to the lavatory.

Chapter Six

When Shiloh suggested growing a garden, I thought she was joking. *Me, plant flowers?* "Pah!" I said. It was the morning after my mother convinced me to move back into the bungalow with her and Ted. I wasn't much in the spirit for growing a garden when I came in. Having told Shiloh about how I'd spent yesterday day-drinking in my childhood bedroom with my mother, I was surprised her solution was to garden.

"What was that, Eva?"

"Pah!" I said again.

To which Shiloh said, "Great. We'll go to the nursery together."

Other than her waist-length mop of blond princess hair, my therapist Shiloh's second most distinctive physical trait was the mole on her cheek, smack dab between her right ear and nostril—the place you'd expect to find a witch's wart or Marilyn Monroe's pencil dot, which hardly qualified as a mole when you compared it to Shiloh's.

"Eva?"

"Mmmm?"

"What do you say we go to the nursery together?"

"The what?" I gaped at her.

I don't know where Shiloh did her clothes shopping, but I had the impression that everything she wore had been tailor made for her. Maybe she was housing a Parisian seamstress in some secret rose-furnished compartment in her office.

Today, her uniform consisted of a pantsuit in the same shade of camel as the leather couch in her office—the one that made me feel like a vagabond whenever I sat down. Shiloh also wore her usual browline glasses, plus a flowy top under the jacket. Boasting ruffles down the front, the blouse seemed to be inspired by the timeless fashion of George Washington.

"That's where you get seeds," Shiloh was saying, inclining her head with that perfect blend of patience and polite concern that made her a princess. "You've never had a garden before?"

"Look, Shiloh," I started. I was beginning to regret unloading yesterday's calamity of margaritas and dolls, the general sense of panic that had seized my mother's bungalow in its claws. "I don't even think my landlady allows flowers. In fact, I think she's anti-botanicals. I mean, I don't have a yard. My whole complex is basically an island of cement."

Actually, the only thing vaguely reminiscent of vegetation was this sheet printed with petunias. The sheet had been hanging on my neighbor's clothesline since the summer before last. When I told Shiloh this, I forwent mentioning my suspicion that the irregular pattern of red blots might have been from someone having bled on the fabric. It had already occurred to me that maybe the sheet was more representative of some ceremonial deflowering than it was of literal blossoms. Why else would my neighbor keep it slung like some triumphant flag over her line? If my neighbor kept it up much longer, I imagine the design would disappear altogether—the red blots on the sheet were already fading. And even before I moved into my cement apartment complex, my knowledge and exposure to flowers was limited. The bungalow had been teeming with golf course-ready grass, yes, but that was it. Other than the hardy geraniums and rhododendrons nestled into the islands dividing Ship Bottom's main strip, the décor of most properties relied on seashell gravel, pinwheel spinners, and anthropomorphic garden statues of hedgehogs and rabbits.

Shiloh studied me with her pretty head tilted, and I studied her back. Because her name is "Shiloh," I couldn't help but think about the coming-of-age story about the boy who takes care of an abused dog—I'm unable to recall the details. I just know my mother adored that beagle. And sometimes when Shiloh looked at me like that, head aslant with her brown eyes wide, I think of the pup in that beloved novel.

Shiloh's cheek mole lifted slightly as she asked, "What about tomatoes?"

"Excuse me?"

"Do you like tomatoes?" Shiloh tucked a strand of princess hair behind her ear. Did she have to remind herself to toss her locks over one shoulder before closing the car door behind her, or was the maneuver so ingrained in her, it had become habit? "Eva? Is there something you—"

"Sure," I bumbled. White spring light was beating into Shiloh's office, making me feel exposed and vulnerable. "Tomatoes, yes. In sauce that's on pasta, it's good." Now why was I talking like my tree topper Yoda?

"Do you like to make pasta?" Shiloh smiled. And because she wears those kinds of glasses that tint upon contact with the sun, I could see the outline of my head reflected balloon-like across them.

"If it already comes with the sauce."

"Well, scratch that." Shiloh scribbled something in the notebook I was beginning to believe was a biological outgrowth of her hand. What was she writing? That I preferred Chef Boyardee's mini cheese raviolis to just about anything else—take that, *Eat Right!*

The hour got swallowed, just as it always did in Shiloh's office. Shiloh would get me going on one topic and I'd fall into it. Falling so hard I forgot what I was saying, or forgot that I wasn't saying anything at all, but staring idiotically down at the floor. And so it wasn't until later, when Shiloh directed our attentions again to the inexhaustible subject of my mother, that I came back to myself, and mentioned her upcoming bridal shower. How it was a handful of the Kaminskis plus Mythic Ethel who would be—

"Mythic Ethel?"

"My great aunt. She's basically a witch. But not the warty kind. More like a religious enchantress with a walker?"

"I see." Shiloh made another note in her book and nodded, adding that she thought this time with my family would be good for me.

"Clearly you don't know them." I smiled wryly.

"But surely it will be good to be around your family. You mentioned you and your cousin Vivian were close as children? Well, perhaps you two can talk to her about Sebasti—"

I turned my mind off to whatever Shiloh said next, because what I'd thought would make me happy was a thing of the past. I'd long ago invited Shiloh to sue me for awakening obsessions on which to pin my pain. It didn't matter that Shiloh kept a subarctic temperature in her office. I sweated torrentially whenever I was there.

"Eva?"

"Yes?" I wiped my sweating brow with the back of my wrist.

"I was just asking if you were still free at our usual time next week?"

Free—me? I wasn't working. I had no friends other than my mother. On the days I wasn't scheduled to appear at Fountain-of-You Yoga or Shiloh's, I was waiting to appear at Fountain-of-You Yoga or Shiloh's. Or streaming *Midsomer Murders.*

I was free as could be, I told Shiloh.

"Good. Do you know the nursery Toadstool & Petals? It isn't far, I'll give you the address and we can meet there. Sound good?"

I nodded, deliciously confused. Because this was so unconventional for a professional princess like Shiloh, I thought it sounded wonderful.

Chapter Seven

When I evolved at *Eat Right!* from coffee vendor to fulltime writer, it didn't matter that I'd told my boss, Olive, I would be tickled to write a tri-quarterly column, knowing nothing about the subject for which I was put in charge. It was the first time I'd been offered a job more involved than pouring her bowel-cleansing coffee. Despite the research I'd initially devoted to being her kale columnist, that sucky vegetable continued to be as fleeting to me as a passing "goodbye" or "hello." That I consented to having my photo accompany my first published column didn't lessen the knockback of the matter. I'd only agreed to stand in front of the camera because I'd thought the photo of my fake-noshing on kale chips would be a one-time thing. Really, I'd done it for the squirrely-faced intern, Kevin, whose suggestion was the first that Olive didn't look like she wanted to clobber the poor guy for making. But the column went over so well that, by some twist of the universe, I acquired a fan base. I thought Olive was kidding when, upon asking if I'd be up for having my portrait *à la kale* taken again. She said, "Readers want to attach a face to the kale—and you, Eva, are that face!"

And that is the story of how every kale column published during my time at *Eat Right!* included not only a bullshit essay composed by yours truly, but a photo of me posing with whatever new recipe the culinary specialists at *Eat Right!* were trying their damnedest to seem appetizing.

All the while, I'd felt like Barbara Stanwyck, who plays the cosmopolitan Elizabeth Lane in the holiday classic *Christmas in Connecticut.* Devising something to say about kale was like snatching for clouds. Clouds upon clouds of smelly kale heads, the leaves evaporating before I could get to them. Except where Elizabeth Lane attempts to faithfully charade a rural life in the romantic write-ups she pens for *Smart Housekeeping*, I wasn't even trying to pull off the farce. Maybe if I'd been given more than one disgusting trend to write about, I might have tried harder. But because my subject was static, its health benefits generic as all get-up, I disguised the fact that I knew nothing about wild cabbage's dirty cousin by insisting how recipe x or y would be the perfect complement to whatever soiree or casual tête–à–tête the readers who took *Eat Right!* for godsend were hosting.

Give me a hairy coconut over a kale rosette any day, and I swear, I'll come up with something nice to say.

After my mother began receiving *Eat Right!*, she'd randomly bring up something I'd written in one of my columns. Though I had been wedded to my mother's side since I was a kid, I was still often thrown back by the unpredictability that characterized her way of thinking.

"Eva," I can remember her regarding me seriously over her cucumber sandwich, holding her pinky finger up like a duchess. We were reposing in the sun, wearing matching fringed kimonos and flip-flops with artificial roses glued to the thongs—accessories my mother had insisted we wear out on the lawn. It must have been the summer before we lost Sebastian, because my mother and I were happy then.

My mother set down her sandwich. "Tell me the truth." She tossed her hair over her shoulder and picked up her sangria. I imagine she must have picked up her sangria, swishing it around. Because that was what Leonora Marino was always doing when she lapsed into the playfulness that made me love her all the more. "Do you actually believe all you say about kale?"

"What do I say about kale?" I said honestly. Having penned at least half a dozen issues by then, kale had become so wedded to my vocabulary I'd lost track of what I'd said about it.

"In every issue, you encourage us to eat more of it," my mother said over my silence. I tended to do that, drift into that ramshackle attic my brain had become. My mother was used to this and recognized the thing to do was to plow on. I'd catch up soon enough. ". . . and then you talk about how it's high in vitamins and anti-inflammatory and basically the ambrosia of the gods." My mother swirled her glass between taking bird-like sips. The sun glimmered off the pieces of gold thread stitching in her kimono. "And so I factored kale into my diet to see what it'd feel like."

"Mom," I snapped into focus. She was chewing her bottom lip with an aggressiveness that was beyond disturbing. I studied the cucumber sandwich I had been in the middle of chewing, identifying the flecks of green I'd seen in the cream cheese. *Gross!* I set down my sandwich, scraped my tongue with my napkin. "Don't pay attention to anything I write in there. It's all nonsense," I said. "Honestly, Mom, I make up half of that stuff you've—"

"Is there such a thing as kale stones?" My mother's eyes widened. "Because I integrated kale into my diet and now that's what I think I've got." My mother ran her pixie-sized hand through her hair. Back then, she wore her bangs long, let her blond locks fall freely from beneath the bucket hat she'd developed a baffling fondness for. It was all straw and fabric flowers—like a garden had been dumped on her head.

"Honey, I think the kale is propagating inside me!" Leonora Marino pulled at her sundress as if it had been infected by the kale she'd ingested. "Like every leaf I've consumed has squeezed another baby kale out, and I've been taking it in by the bushel!"

If I was a hashtag aficionado like my mother, I might have tweeted:

#NotYourAverageKaleExpert
#cleaneatingnomnom

I'd been prepared to quit my job at *Eat Right!* altogether, but my boss, Olive, insisted I take the spring off and return in the summer. "We'll already be planning next winter's edition by then! Imagine: Christmas Kale Salad! Garlicky Kale-Stuffed Chicken! Meatball-Kale Minestrone!"

"Olive," I put a hand out to stop her. Imagined the gorge, and Sebastian's face in the water. Sebastian hitting rock bottom.

"What is it, Eva? Too far with the minestrone? I know it has a reputation for—"

I told Olive I thought I was going to puke, and I did, right then and there, on Olive's open-toe espadrilles.

When I returned from the bathroom, my computer had already been logged out, a box packed with my desk stuff, and the entire art department was damp with the smell of disinfectant.

I had thought that taking a break from work would soothe me. That not having to slip outside to hide that I was lunching on cheddar popcorn and Twizzlers, and not some gluten-free pita pocket stuffed with a mush of soybeans and sprouts, would take a load off. Instead, the very opposite was true. For while I did find some satisfaction in turning down the blinds and balling up on the couch, watching back-to-back episodes of *Midsomer Murders*, this was not enough to curb the anxiety of thinking. Not having a routine afforded me more time to think. And contrary to the popular notion, having time on your hands to live in your head was not necessarily a good condition.

Not, at least, when the only subject you could think about was the very thing you were trying to escape.

It was after screening more seasons of *Midsomer Murders* than I care to admit that I decided I needed to do something more to occupy my time than seeing Shiloh, tending to my mother's beck and call, and pressing into downward dog at Fountain-of-You Yoga. I had begun to seriously wonder who in their right mind would choose to live in the villages of Midsomer, and how there were even any villagers left alive to prey on. With every episode heralding a new pitchfork and scythe murder for Detective Barnaby and Sergeant Troy to track, it seemed like the entire town should have been a bloodbath.

For the kale column *Eat Right!* published before I took my leave of absence, I was asked to pose with a platter of kale and goat cheese-stuffed poblanos. Olive had even asked that I wear a black cocktail dress, and because Olive had consented to my taking a paid leave, I'd said yes.

Cocktail dresses were not my thing.

To make matters worse, some nitwit in the airbrush department thought it would be a good idea to draw out the color saturation in the photo, and thereby dramatize the contrast between the dress and my skin. This destroyer of what morsels of self-respect I had left had even gone as far as to Photoshop steam rising from the poblanos.

Of course, Leonora Marino loved it: "Eva in her LBD!" she tweeted my column.

Chapter Eight

Because I'd stopped keeping a plan book and refrained from jotting down anything other than my reflections in the journal I was supposed to be keeping, I forgot I was supposed to meet Shiloh at the nursery. The reflections I wrote down for Shiloh included fragments about the daily weather—*Seafoam sky, heat lightning fizzing like pop rocks*—and sometimes a detailed description of the porridge whose dredges I'd left crusting the bowl—*Color like smoked truffles, scaly texture. Do I spy a spume of mold?*

And so it wasn't until I arrived at her office, pumped to sweat atop her leather couch, per usual, that I recalled we'd changed our meeting spot. I must have flown to the nursery in a brownout. I was only ten-minutes late by the time I arrived. According to my GPS, it should have taken me twice as long to reach the nursery.

Toadstool & Petals hummed the way I imagined Hades' underworld kingdom might have smelled when he snatched Persephone, which is to say, like a bedchamber of honey and loam.

Because Shiloh is a princess, she forgave me right away.

"It happened, it's over." Her cheek mole rose as she smiled. She was wearing a sunhat and a floral-print maxi dress that swirled in the wind. She definitely had a secret fairy helping her pick out her clothes; how else to explain her capacity to coordinate so perfectly with her surroundings?

"You needn't be nice on my account." I shoved my hands into the pockets of my sweatpants. Was that a cheese curl I felt?

Shiloh was not deterred from her abundant fount of kindness.

"Here, look at these Asiatic lilies," she pushed the blooms into my face.

Shadowing Shiloh through the aisles of the nursery, feeling out of my element surrounded by plants about which I knew nothing, I tried to mirror what Shiloh was doing. Reading the care instructions for some, breathing in the heady fragrance of others. At one point, she picked up a pot of God-knows-what. The leaves seemed furry, like something that belonged on the head of a Muppet.

"Don't worry," Shiloh laughed when she saw me eyeing the fronds. "This isn't for you, it's for my son. Valentine loves lamb's ear—ever seen one?"

I shook my head, not even bothering to hide the glance I shot at Shiloh's left hand. I hadn't thought to look for a ring. Was there one?

"Here, feel."

The lamb's ear was indeed fleecy, its texture similar to that of those lucky rabbit's foot keychains the tourists who visited Ship Bottom every summer cleaned out of Hoy's 5&10. It was not uncommon to find a neon-blue rabbit's foot smooshed on the side of the road, or a hot pink one half-hidden under a dune. Maybe the luck associated with the keychains pertained to the feet themselves. Their capacity to separate themselves from their owners.

"You can get one, too, if you like!" beamed Shiloh, who'd clearly understood the expression conveyed by my wandering thoughts for enthusiasm for that pot. I was not covetous of Valentine's lamb's ear, however. What I wanted to know was why I couldn't just pin myself down in the present.

"That's okay." I retracted my hand.

"What do you say we go look at the seeds?" Shiloh indicated a rack of seed packets. I saw then, that Shiloh was not wearing a wedding band.

I ended up leaving the nursery with a carrier of nutrient-rich soil and a variety of seed packets, a small watering can that Shiloh picked out, and a coffee plant whose deep green leaves looked severe and oily, like maybe they contained hallucinogenic properties.

We were carrying our loot back to the parking lot when the sun dipped behind the clouds and the sky grew dark. I could feel the beginnings of a migraine take root.

"See you back at my office next time?" Shiloh called at the same moment the wind picked up, sending the leaves of my coffee plant flapping.

"Definitely!" I shouted over the gusts.

I found the five missed calls from my mother after I slid into my Honda and the rain began to bullet down. Her most recent text read, *Eva, the shower is tomorrow. And it looks like a storm is a-brewing—isn't it wonderful? April showers bring May flowers . . . and a wedding for your mother. LOL! This is both a reminder and an S.O.S.! xoxo YOUR MOTHER*

Chapter Nine

I look back on my childhood, and what I see first is a fortress of books. We had so many in the house, I used some of them as building blocks for my castles and forts. My mother's comparison of our shared reality to storybook plots did not take away my enthusiasm for books. If anything, it augmented it, and made novels and poems so much a part of my childhood consciousness that I have a hard time not comparing my reality to things I experienced through reading.

It was no wonder my mother and Finn were so tight: though his house was roughly the size of a breadbox in comparison to ours, it too was packed to the gills with books. While Dad was away in the winter, they staged abridged performances of Shakespeare's plays for Sebastian and me. My mother switching between Hermia and Helena, Portia and Calpurnia; blending Rosencrantz and Guildenstern into one sod of a compatriot to Finn's portrayal of Hamlet. My mother and Finn even went so far as to shroud the furniture in spooky cheesecloth for *Macbeth*; for the final act of *The Merry Wives of Windsor,* Finn strew the living room with tinsel-wrapped branches and wildflowers suspiciously similar to those in the beds decorating Ship Bottom's pedestrian center.

I can remember my parents arguing into the night one winter Dad returned from his travels earlier than we expected. In those days, I'd misunderstood the heart of their quarrelling, and oftentimes would come down in my nightgown to sidle up to my mother, prepared to defend her. After all, I was disposed to be closer to her; with Dad away vending his clocks at flea markets, I was with Leonora Marino an entire season more than I was with him.

The winter Dad came back before we were prepared for his

return, I listened from the stairwell, my forehead pressing the slats of the bannister, as my mother paced and smashed things. Dad said something that made my mother go bananas—that was always how it happened. Dad would say something and that made my mother lose it.

This time, the evidence of our fun-making was evinced in the living room. My mother and I hadn't yet cleaned up the home theatre she and Finn had transformed it into. Witches' hats and capes, fairy wings and prop swords covered the floors. I can still see the ketchup-stained dishrag left carelessly on the sofa. The sullying of that dishrag all in the interest of creating a prop worthy of Lady Macbeth. And I can remember being disappointed in Dad for being testy with my mother at what I supposed to be toward the general mess. It was no biggie, the motel staff would swing by to clean up like always—Mom was just having fun, Dad. Come on.

In fonder times, Dad called my mother "Panda" because of the dark circles around her eyes. He meant it as a compliment, I think, pandas being pretty much unanimously cute, if not vicious when it comes to hoarding bamboo. It was only during the years Dad was alive that my mother bore those darkly ringed eyes. I never realized, then, how that period coincided with the one during which Finn and Sebastian lived in town. In hindsight, it's only fair to mention that my mother's eyes also bore dark circles during the span when they were around.

My mother has gotten thinner and potentially crazier since Dad's death. The purple shadows that once ghosted her eyes have been replaced by crow's feet, folds she insists on calling laugh lines. "Because life is a joke!" she'd gloat on the days I could tell it took an effort for her to put on a face and act as if everything was okay.

So it was that on the surface, my parents were all goo. Between the ludicrously popular motel line Dad inherited when his father died and the money my mother's parents mailed without an explanation to Dad—as if that chunk of change signified their downfallen daughter's dowry—my parents and I could live like kings and queens.

In reality, however, when it came to facing the everyday, Dad and my mother were not the peas in a pod they tried to sell to Ship Bottom. A business man and a restless entrepreneur, Dad tried to carry on his father's business while making and marketing the elaborate cuckoo clocks he was obsessed with. Manning the motels in the summer while he golfed and assembled his designs required no small amount of his time, and while he was busy extending my deceased grandfather's legacy by renovating and boosting the popularity of the famed Ship Bottom motels, my mother was busy rebelling against her parents. She did this by marrying my father and having a daughter before the clock they'd wound for her said it was time. This, in their eyes, my mother's worst crime.

Before I could act like a semi-functioning person, my mother turned me over to a governess. Miss Wimple was all rosy-face and bosom. I don't remember her, of course, but I have seen old home videos of me being bounced around by a woman who looks like she stepped straight out of an illustrated book of children's verse. She was Mother Hubbard, kind and without children of her own. A part of my infancy and a part of how I understood how my mother once regarded me when I was a baby.

Later, when I came across the tapes of me with Miss Wimple, and jokingly accused my mother of hocking me off to a bosomy old woman, my mother compared the arrangement to the one Shakespeare's Juliet had with her wet nurse: "Every woman should have a wet nurse," my mother insisted—even though her terminology was misleading because Miss Wimple was far past the age for which it was biologically possible for her to nurse me.

No sooner did I learn how to talk than my mother relieved Miss Wimple and took to her garbling daughter. By then, I was no longer a mound of crying flesh with needs, but a tiny human who could speak.

One day, my mother says to me on one of the old video tapes, *I'll teach you to read, Eva.*

It seems clear to me now that the moment my mother realized what she had—that her daughter would be her forever friend—I became for her a wondrous little person. No one else would ever measure up to her Eva. From what I could glean, my mother only passed me along to Miss Wimple because Leonora Marino did not know how to handle a human needier than she.

Leonora Marino wanted to be a children's librarian but had absolutely no experience working either at a library or with multiple children. So, once I was stable enough not to bonk my head on every surface I met, my mother started volunteering at the local children's library. She'd deposit me in one of those cages masquerading as playpens, then go about her duties, which consisted of reading stories during circle time and distributing graham crackers and milk cartons to her rapt audience.

Children adored my mother, who I couldn't imagine resembled their own mothers at all. Leonora Marino was all raucous color, an exotic bird. A charmer of children as well as men. Where women of all ages balked at her spiritedness, men took to Leonora like moths to coat closets, flapping passionately toward a dark warmth that they could lose themselves in.

I think the degree with which my mother appreciated children's stories owed to the typicality of their endings. Like puzzles you can depend on to come together, the plots my mother adored were the ones that best normalized problems, made answers of fables. In the end, readers were granted the opportunity to make meaning from the confusion of life. For that, I believe she was glad. If Nancy Drew could bring order to the world, my mother could, too.

Chapter Ten

The morning my bride-to-be mother was expecting the clan, she phoned in a stitch. "Eva, I need you!"

That was all she had to say for me to nab my car keys and pack my things.

When I arrived, the living room looked like Hallmark and Michael's Craft Store had gotten together and had a baby. There was a bowl of blood-red punch in the corner reminiscent of the Ides of March fountain of gore Calpurnia goes on about in *Julius Caesar.* The curls of ribbon and cloth petals reminded me of my dead cat Buttermilk. When Buttermilk wasn't sleeping or molesting my face with her velvety paws, she liked to knead my doors and walls. The day I came home to discover my carpet looking like it had a nasty case of dandruff, plaster from Buttermilk's scratch-fest snowing the floor, I knew my cat had destroyed any chance of my getting my security deposit back when I moved. Which was, I reminded myself, all too soon.

"Eva, you coming?"

After she insisted I sample a pig knuckle dumpling she'd ordered from some Polish mail-order company—it was basically a ready-to-serve heart attack my mother nuked and delivered to me on a plate she'd garnished with clippings she'd gathered from goodness-knows-where—my mother asked me to help her decide on an appropriate bridal shower outfit. While I was sitting on the end of her bed, trying to coax Caboodle the Shih Tzu to walk across the iron head board without falling sideways like the oversized cotton swab he was, my mother brought Sebastian up.

"I can hardly believe Sebastian's gone," she said as she slipped into yet another of her tent-like dresses that were all so baggy and shapeless and strange. I was sure it was only a matter of time before a herd of dwarves came strolling out from under the hem.

I jumped as Caboodle lunged at the rail and promptly fell off. Cradling him to my chest, I adjusted the yellow ribbons my mother had bowed about each ear. Caboodle was panting heavily from his failed effort as I tried to shield my face with his fur.

"So often I think of him," my mother was saying, "of how you and he should be making a mess together, like when you were kids. Do you remember the time Sebastian . . ."

"Oh, that looks nice, Mom!" I pointed to the necklace in her hand, a string of glass bobbles reminiscent of human eyeballs. I dropped Caboodle on the bed and stepped into my mother's walk-in closet. "I'll see if I can't find something to go with it."

I could hear Caboodle sneezing on himself and the swish of my mother poking through her dish of earrings as I tried to swallow the lump in my throat. At the back of her clothes rack, a blouse caught my eye. The ivory silk was rumpled, like the blouse had been fisted into a ball before someone showed mercy and decided to hang it up.

"What about this?" I carried it out.

The Venetian blinds' grid of light and shadow made bars across my mother's face. She held the blouse out at arm's length as she gestured to a stain: "Oh, Eva."

It was hard to take my mother seriously when she was standing half dressed, bony hip cocked to one side talking to me so loud she was nearly shouting. "Why would I wear something so dated? That thing is a decade or more past its prime!" She flung the blouse and threw up her hands.

I wanted to wrap my arms around her and tell her how senseless I thought she was becoming, but no sooner had I returned the blouse to her closet than the doorbell rang, Caboodle started barking, and as my mother struggled to yank one of her bag dresses back over her head, I kept my mouth shut and helped her. I knew that as far as my feelings for my mother were concerned, it was always my tenderness for her that won.

Chapter Eleven

My mother owned a share of her parents' camp in Maine, and it was at this camp that one week in July, Finn and Sebastian joined my parents and me.

Sebastian and I had seen some things that final summer we were together as kids. We saw Finn fondling my mother's breasts, and later that day, or that week, we saw my parents standing on either side of the open dishwater as they piled clean dishes inside it.

Sebastian and I didn't talk about it afterward. Instead, we crossed the marshy footbridge and forged a path through the thickets of witch grass. Eventually tumbling down to the shore, where we came upon a crate floating at the edges of the surf. Inside, rock crabs quivered in a stack—there must have been a few dozen, the ones on top foaming at the mouth when we opened the crate. Because their claws were secured with plastic twine, we took turns lifting one out at a time, cutting it free, and giving it back to the sea.

When we returned to Ship Bottom, my parents told me to take a seat at the table.

I don't remember much of what my mother said after she delivered the news while Dad stared straight ahead, like he was trying to read a message etched into the wallpaper.

While I waited for my mother to stop talking, I dug my fingernails into my shorts. When she and Dad eventually left, I remained at the table picking at the Jordan Almonds left over from some long-forgotten party. Some households kept fresh fruit on their tables, but at the Marino household, we kept bowls of stale candies and nuts. Mostly, they were left untouched; picked at only when someone was distracted or, in my case, under duress.

When I went to look for Sebastian, I found him slumped in the chipped Adirondack chair behind his cottage. I can remember Sebastian was wearing his Kurt Cobain t-shirt because his hands were arranged over Kurt Cobain's mouth, like Kurt had some big secret that Sebastian was ill at ease at the prospect of revealing.

When I mentioned our moving, Sebastian told me to *Stop it Stop it Stop it.*

I climbed into the chair with him, and for a while we listened to the cars turn down the road, the drone of a mower triming one among the perfect lawns on our block.

I was fourteen-years-old at the time, and sure Sebastian and I would never see one another again. But like children in fairy stories who think they've lost their way when in reality, their falling apart is only the trigger for some second beginning or terrible misfortune—I could not have fathomed what our futures had in store.

Chapter Twelve

Justina didn't have a car, which is why she had me hop on the tandem bike she shared with her boyfriend Fabian so we could make a quick zip to The Mystic Mermaid and back—The Mystic Mermaid was the farthest of my parents' motels from our bungalow. And, to put it as vaguely as Justina, there was something Justina needed to do.

The big surprise?

Justina and I weren't the only ones in the unmade guest room, which my mother had had redecorated with seafoam carpet, palm tree wallpaper, and bedside lamps shaped like shells. We found Daria balled up in the garden tub in the bathroom, a screen of cigarette smoke, the skirt of her blue and white pinstriped jumper spread around her.

Looking back, I wish I'd asked more questions. Knowing more about how others managed the day-to-day might have helped prepare me for the wider world. But walking in on Daria puffing her Pall Mall in the tub seemed so natural to Justina, I pretended the image was no big deal to me, either.

As Justina joined Daria in a cigarette and perched on the toilet seat lid—another surface my mother had adorned with seafoam shag—I leaned against the bathroom door, transfixed by how comfortable and mature Justina and Daria were. And because my mother had seen to filling my adolescent closet with magenta denim that featured spatters of glitter across the pockets, you can imagine how I looked alongside gorgeous Justina, who made straddling the plush lid of a motel john look attractive.

Justina began talking to Daria in Polish, the hand that wasn't pinching her cigarette gesticulating wildly to illustrate whatever narrative Daria listened to in earnest. When Daria, wet-eyed from laughing, interrupted Justina to offer me a drag from her "ciggy," I turned on my flip-flop and tuck-jumped onto the California King to wait until Justina emerged, gave the duvet and pillows a fluff, and it was time to go home.

After that, I began hanging out with more of my parents' staff, who eventually became somewhat of a life force to me. Particularly by the time I returned to Ship Bottom during the summers I attended Moore Hedge, when Sebastian and Finn had already moved and I began to consult Justina and Daria as friends.

It's been some years since I saw them last. After Dad passed, my mother had to lay off most of the hired help to makes ends meet, which explains how her bungalow became a mess, as well as the onslaught of sanitation-related comments Dad's motel guests had posted to TripAdvisor before my mother sold the motels in favor of "shutting them down forever."

Of the many comments decrying Dad's once revered motels, the one I remembered most was reminiscent of an undergraduate persuasive essay written under the influence of boxed wine. I imagine it had been composed by a recent PhD graduate, however; one who had taught one-too-many sections of freshman composition. The guest's username was "DrJoeDigstheBrontës," and his dictum I bookmarked on my web browser:

Don't be duped by The Pugnacious Pirate's rates—no Jolly Roger is worth sleeping in kids' skull and crossbones sheets or washing in a shower with a rusted captain's wheel.

There's sand in the carpet, too. I felt like Chuck Noland marooned on an island. My Dover edition of Wuthering Heights *was my sole totem of comfort, basically my Wilson. LOL.*

My discomfort only increased upon finding a sock in my pillowcase. Moreover, there were rustling noises in the walls and the portrait of Blackbeard looked like it was done by a kindergartener, and not in a quaint way.

To conclude, I think the Pugnacious Pirate is haunted and I caution you to stay away.

According to my mother, her having to fire over half her Polish staff reflected her "profoundest grief"—after Dad's death, that is.

I never told anyone the things Sebastian and I saw transpire between our parents. Not even Shiloh knew the extent of my mother's infidelity, though I suppose she could guess. Or, perhaps, in the appointments I was almost sure she was also attending, my mother had confessed.

Looking back, what had once felt like some big, unspoken secret, must have been obvious. I wouldn't have been surprised to learn that Justina and Daria and the rest had known what my mother and Finn were doing as fact: my mother didn't disguise the act when Dad was away. It was almost as if my mother put on a show for the bungalow's eyes alone. How many times had Sebastian and I watched her and Finn, pressed together in a romantic embrace, from the large bay window at the top of the bungalow's staircase?

The first time Sebastian and I caught his father kissing my mother in the garden was viewed from this same window—my mother in her floppy bonnet, Finn's face partially obscured by its brim.

I wonder if it hurts, Sebastian had said, meaning his dad's scruff. I imagined it didn't matter how often his father took up a razor; Finn was one of those men with a permanent five o'clock shadow.

Sebastian and I had probably been about seven and five at the time, and I can recall the way Sebastian's brow furrowed, how his lower lip trembled in wonderment. You had to hand it to Sebastian to exude such concern at that age.

And so, whereas children's books seemed to balance the world for my mother, so too did relationships with Dad and Finn regulate Sebastian's and my understanding of her. My mother was just a sexual being, we decided, as soon as Sebastian heard the word "sex" from a second-grade classmate and then explained to me, the kindergartener, what the act meant:

It's all about the birds and the bees.

"The birds and the bees?"

The birds and the bees, Sebastian nodded resolutely.

Indeed, my mother was so busy ignoring what she did, I eventually saw her lack of action when it came to telling me things as qualifiers for her behavior. In the midst of her overt sensuality, she never did give me "the talk."

Chapter Thirteen

The bell was still ringing when I opened the door.

Towering on the porch was Uncle Tuck in an orange hunting cap and Aunt Ginny lugging some kind of casserole that looked heavy enough to kill.

"Hello!" I put on my best smile as I shepherded them in.

In their shearling-lined coats and muffs, it was like my uncle and aunt wanted to eternally live in the skin of animals. It was 70-degrees out! Did the fact that they were from the Pennsylvania Dutch region of Lancaster predispose them to always bundle themselves in their woolens?

"We're on that California kick," Uncle Tuck explained, registering the confused judgment my face must have betrayed.

"You know, the one where people wear trash bags," added Aunt Ginny.

"Of course!" I nodded and feigned understanding. Because obviously the Golden State, known for its showbiz and surfers, LA Fitness and the Manson murders, was the source behind the "kick" to which Uncle Tuck referred. I'd heard of wearing trash bags to the gym to increase your body temperature, sure. But woolens to a springtime family weekend, celebrating the impending marriage of my mother? My uncle and aunt looked ridiculous and the shininess of their foreheads made me uncomfortable. I could only imagine how much of Aunt Ginny's sweat had ended up in whatever casserole she'd brought. Ginny Kaminski prided herself on her casseroles. In fact, I don't think I'd ever eaten anything she'd made that did not come in either casserole or Jell-O form, or somehow involve mayonnaise and mounds of meat molded into animal shapes. It was distressing on so many levels.

I inhaled strong wafts of Aunt Ginny's casserole as I made to follow them into the kitchen, only to promptly turn around, taking the opportunity of their distraction to rest my head against the foyer wall.

I hadn't seen any of my mother's family since they'd piled into the parlor for Dad's funeral. They herded in, rather. They had been dressed appropriately in black, but unfortunately, they all smelled like wood chips and tent canvas. Ginny descended from a long line of camping enthusiasts, which explained why her bright red bob perpetually smelled of a fire pit. The only fragments of the Kaminskis I recall from that day were Uncle Tuck shoveling deviled eggs in his mouth at the reception; my cousin Vivian digging her kitten heel into the floor as she studied the collage my mother had made, sticky-tacking washed-out family photos to a posterboard.

While Ginny took off for the kitchen, pushing through the confusion of luggage and casserole, Uncle Tuck thumped me on the back and told me what a sturdy girl I was. "Seriously, Eva. You could knock some poor ass out—*bam*!"

Knock some poor ass out: that is just what I wanted to do to my Uncle Tuck if he called me a "sturdy girl" again.

Entering the kitchen at the same moment, Uncle Tuck hustled after Aunt Ginny and her casserole, preying upon her with some joke or other. I remembered then why I recognized the blouse I'd found at the back of my mother's closet. It was recalling how the stain upset her that made me suddenly remember.

My mother had worn the blouse, I think, at one of my parents' New Year's Eve parties—an annual to-do that a decade or more before necessitated Sebastian and I stay in the basement with the other neighborhood kids, while upstairs, the adults drank and played elaborate games of charades.

I am almost certain my mother had been wearing that blouse on one of those nights, pouring glasses of wine for everyone when Dad must have said something—a joke, Sebastian and I'd heard him shouting later in his defense—that somehow ended in my mother covered in wine.

Sebastian and I had been in the basement and hadn't witnessed the incident itself. We'd heard the commotion, though. The raised voices and breaking glass, the front door opening and closing. The ball had dropped and the dawn of a new year seemed to be swell, so far. But upstairs, no one seemed to care that the world had not ended, after all.

My parents had never been good at keeping their emotions reigned in. Dad wore his irritation on his cuff like an expensive watch my mother was always reminding him to wind, but she—though the more ardent of my parents—couldn't come close to shocking me in the way that Dad did that night. It was after all the parents came to collect the neighborhood kids that I noticed him in the kitchen. I had tiptoed up to use the bathroom when I found him standing in front of the dishwasher. Dad, with his eyes closed and his head tilted back while my mother in her stained blouse knelt before him, her head jerking against his beltline.

When I returned to the basement, Sebastian wasn't the least fazed by my story.

It's okay, he whispered, taking my hands in his. His eyes shone at me in the dark. *Your parents are good people. They wouldn't do anything to hurt each other.*

My parents' parties continued long after they deemed Sebastian and me old enough to attend them. All of them, I quickly observed, began the same way: my mother darting between bartending and endless rounds of charades while Dad ferried the platters of mini meatballs and cheese puffs Justina made from room to room. My parents solicited Justina's and Daria's help for certain matters, but never asked that they be present to assist with their parties. At the end of most of these evenings, my parents fought. At many of them, Finn and my mother were only cordial with one another. They pretended to only be friends.

My cousins Vivian and Charlize arrived, and let me tell you, it was a disquieting experience to whirl around and find Charlize's face pressed against the windowpane alongside the doorway. Her nose smoothed the glass with an alien interest, Gulliver peering in at the Lilliputians.

Vivian actually named her daughter after the actress Charlize Theron, whose performance in *Mighty Joe Young* was apparently enough to have earned her forename a place on our family tree. After seeing the actress play the serial killer in *Monster*, however, I couldn't help but feel sorry for Vivian's daughter, whose shrewd perception of human nature made her something of a monster. I can remember three-year-old Charlize asking her mother if she might please have some shrimp cocktail like the grownups, "I'm not much a fan of chocolate. It made Grandma like that, don't you see?" This anecdote only makes sense if you know that my aunt is a diabetic, and also stricken by a variety of dissimilar ailments.

On that same family occasion, my second-cousin had also, after watching Aunt Ginny inject herself with insulin, asked my aunt if she was administering Novocain. "Are you trying to stop the pain of your sugar-cravings, Grandma?"

Following me into the foyer, Vivian flashed me a small smile before looking quickly away. Had the expression I had arranged on my face, hoping it would seem optimistic and upbeat, offended Vivian? Made her turn in order to avoid the horror of looking at her cousin with whom she had been close?

When Vivian and I were children, Aunt Ginny had insisted on dressing us in matching outfits whenever our families got together. It didn't take much convincing when we were tots, and our brains were not yet developed enough to communicate our disdain through anything other than, at least in my case, what I understood to be elusive attempts at the stink face. Ginny kept an entire album of these photos of Vivian and me in our lacy blouses and Bertha collars, plunked in the garden or among my mother's dolls. In all the photos, we look sort of plopped down, like Aunt Ginny had hauled us into the bushiest part of her periwinkle blue hydrangeas to deposit us. Had the photos of me and Vivian been black and white, even sepia, I wouldn't doubt that Aunt Ginny would be able to market them to Cracker Barrel, whose aesthetic seems founded on random Victorians grimacing from funereal clothing, not to mention nostalgic board games and defunct farm equipment transposed from some calloused hand to be strung above Cracker Barrel's diners. The décor had always seemed very threatening to me, and I often wondered if the grits didn't perhaps contain particles of foreign substances in the genera of animal bone or glass.

Anyway, Aunt Ginny's efforts to transform her daughter and me into identical Victorian Stepfords came to a halt when my mother told Aunt Ginny that her presents of bloomers and bonnets had to stop. She was not going to have her daughter dressing like one of her dolls. And so I segued into wearing backwards baseball caps, striped stockings, and t-shirts that said things like "WHERE'S THE PARTY?"

It was in the awkward silence that followed my offering to take Charlize's backpack—a proposal Charlize refused with a forbidding shake of the head—that my mother came fluttering down the staircase in her most vibrant tunic to date. Clearly, she had been waiting until we were all assembled in the foyer to make her triumphant appearance. She blew kisses in the air, feigning humility and outright lying to the group after Aunt Ginny told my mother she looked terrific. "Well, I feel like a clown. I don't normally wear makeup!"

Leonora Marino was one of those women who, in the panache of actresses in Turner Classics, wore makeup to bed. As if she were afraid some disaster might befall her in the middle of the night, chasing her from her bed and into the streets. Heaven forbid she be found without her best face on.

I watched my mother put up a playful attempt at a fight while Uncle Tuck hoisted her up and spun her around, because that's what Uncle Tuck's and my mother's relationship was founded on—acting like animals in Ship Bottom's waning population of wetlands.

When the distress of that was over, my mother asked me to help her with the fruitcake. I wasn't sure why my mother suggested we serve our guests fruitcake then, when I knew she ordered the loaves in bulk, only to freeze them. Thawing them one by one each year at Christmas. When she brought the loaves to gatherings, she did not correct those who complimented her on her baking, and ignored those who asked for the cake recipe. Her go-to tactic was to turn her nose up and ask where the Charles Dickens was the eggnog.

But I wasn't about to question Leonora Marino when her bridal shower had yet to officially kick off.

Uncle Tuck was flinging his piece of fruitcake apart and winking at Charlize to perhaps show he could be a kid, too. Only Charlize seemed more content to pointedly ignore him, conveying that this seven-year-old was not impressed. In fact, she was very busy in extracting the candied fruit from her share of the cake, stacking pieces on the side of her plate.

I knew Vivian had a mouth like nobody's business, and it was not uncommon for my cousin to drop the f-bomb. Had the foul language she'd spouted when we were teenagers begun from an attempt to compensate for Lancaster's abundance of Amish? That is, of reputably being the hotspot for large families of which one's sex was determined by hairnets and long skirts or top hats and sideburns?

I gleaned from Dad's funeral, at which Vivian and Charlize had sat stone-faced in the pews, that motherhood had clearly changed Vivian, who I imagined must have felt compelled to make over her vocabulary so Charlize wouldn't pick up on her ways. Had Dad's passing taken place before Charlize came into the world, I don't doubt that Vivian would have managed to find some occasion that necessitated her to shout the Lord's name out at his funeral reception. "Holy Christ, the chicken salad sandwiches are already gone?"

Meanwhile, my mother filled everyone in on Ted Turbine, whom she described as "la crème de la crème of businessmen," notably neglecting to specify the line of business. And as she went on about the wedding, I thought about how strange it was that my mother used her homemade quilts, carefully patched together from scraps from my old middle school sweatshirts and jeans, to cover up the places on the wall where the wallpaper was peeling. She was so good at spending money, I couldn't imagine why she didn't just hire a painter. Instead she opted to adorn the room where people gathered to commune over food with vestiges of my childhood.

Around the time I was thinking this, I noticed that Vivian was still looking expectantly at me. Like I was the Mona Lisa and Vivian was waiting for me to smile.

I could tell Uncle Tuck had been tempted to make jokes about Ted Turbine since he arrived. Nonsense along the lines of Ted Turbine being a gravedigger and my mother a cradle robber, for

Uncle Tuck had a knack for making jokes eons past the point of cliché actually sound funny. I'd notice the side of his mouth twitch like he was going to say something whenever my mother brought up Ted Turbine. But then, just as quickly, he'd resort to filling his mouth with more fruitcake or catch the look on my face, stop himself, and smirk. I was glad that he'd resisted making those sorts of jokes at the table. Leonora Marino actually seemed relatively content, a spell I knew wouldn't last. We had to enjoy it while we could. There ought to be a write-up in the paper if the weekend passed without conflict. There were far too many personalities under one roof for calamity not to be in the forecast.

As everyone prepared to shift the catching up into the living room, where the bungalow's profusion of luxe Crate & Barrel couches and poufs made it possible to stretch out "like old farts," as Uncle Tuck said, I tried not to embarrass myself.

Let it go, Eva, I thought.

And then I remembered Uncle Tuck's comment about how we were stretched out. It was as if I could no longer see clearly whenever I was in a roomful of people, almost as if I were viewing the world through cloudy goggles.

I was casting my attention about for something to distract me when I noticed Vivian staring at me again. I tried smiling—purposefully raising the edges of my mouth in an approximation of a friendly mien. Only once again, Vivian looked away. But in the brief moment that I was able to catch her eye, I revised the impression I had of her expression. What I had earlier interpreted as disapproval I now realized was more complicated than that. In a glance, what Vivian's face communicated to me was something between fear and pity.

Chapter Fourteen

Ever since the spring we lost Sebastian, I'd gotten into the habit of waking in a cold sweat sometime around dawn. In dreams, I'd see Sebastian and forget he was dead. The wrongness of which propelled me to get out for a walk, shake the dream off. I'd throw on whatever was closest, or, on lazier mornings, wrap myself in the housecoat I lived in whenever my schedule did not necessitate my leaving the comforts of my apartment. I'd get out, breezing past the units on the slab of concrete that distinguished my complex.

In an attempt not to think about the reason for which I'd woken up, I'd invent stories about my neighbors inspired by what they put in their windows. You can tell a lot about a person by what they put in their windows. Or make guesses, anyhow. A towel with the Superman logo covered a third-story pane, behind which I could not help but imagine some tubby teenager who passed his evenings jerking off to the likes of Lois Lane.

That there was hardly anyone around when I went on my walks was the best part. Those I did come upon were always the same, and became part of my walking routine. In terms of wildlife, there were the gulls swooping through the trees. The sad one-eyed tabby I'd find stalking the cattails like he was aiming to be ironic. Then, there was the gentleman I'd encounter at the end of the complex walking his rabbit. Yes, a rabbit. All white fur and piercing red eyes in the style of the chapterbook rabbit. In the series, Bunnicula's adventures revolve around feasting on the juices of vegetables. It's all incredibly exciting, and one of the volumes even makes celery seem almost appealing.

~~~

My parents had been married for a shade over two decades by the time the doctor diagnosed Dad's heart disease, and I suspect my mother and Dad would both agree the period leading up to his diagnosis was the happiest and most painful of their lives—and this was accounting for an entire marriage of unhappiness. They'd stuck together through the rumble of my childhood, as if determined to surpass everyone's expectations.

In the winter months, when it would snow for so long and hard while Dad was well and away selling his clocks, my mother and I would pad ourselves in sweaters and hack away at the ice until Finn, like some god come down from the mountain, appeared out of nowhere, his ginger-blond beard dusted in snow.

My mother eventually hired a guy with a snowplow, but that didn't stop her from calling on Finn whenever so much as a faucet in the bungalow dripped. Leonora Marino and I spent as many hours of the periods Dad was away at Finn and Sebastian's cottage as Finn and Sebastian spent at our bungalow—Finn and my mother huddled before a roaring fireplace, drinking fancy cocoas with little red stirrers, while Sebastian and I hid away from my mother's giggling up in his room.

I can remember once, when the school district dismissed early for ice, Sebastian and I walked the slippery blocks back to the bungalow and stripped out of our coats and galoshes.

After we'd clamored up the stairs, we dove into my bed. Barely breathing as we lay under the covers, quiet and still, our shoulders and hips pressed together. Sebastian having watched a documentary about how to keep alive in various catastrophes, he summarized the main takeaway for me—to keep warm, humans could transmit their body heat by pressing their bodies together, so Sebastian suggested he and I try doing the same.

Who is to say how time really worked in one's childhood? Because when I look back, the memories of undressing and lying gently beside Sebastian extended for weeks. In reality, I imagine we only did this on a handful of occasions.
~~~

What I remember clearly is that one thing led to another, and once we started exploring one another's bodies, it was hard to stop. When we were done, we were always hungry, and one time when we were fixing to cook something, we heard a noise coming from the attic.

We took to what we saw with an almost scientific interest. Conferring, afterwards, that the two things we had discerned upon cracking open the door and shutting it softly behind us were my mother's legs protruding from under the covers of an old cot, while lying on top of her, Sebastian's father shook and shook.

Walking my apartment complex before most of Ship Bottom had yet to wake up became a lifeline to me. Especially on the mornings I was successful at canceling out the negative thoughts that, on the worst days, made even the most mindless tasks seem insurmountable. I was just going through the motions, getting through the day as if every hour was spent underwater. On a logical level I knew I could do something as simple as get out of bed, but then the thought carried the burden of impossibility. Like disbelieving in an anaconda's ability to gulp down a wild boar until, thanks to a late-night Google search, you watch it happen for yourself.

The grounds surrounding my complex had been under construction since the day I moved in; crossing them midway through my walks was something like navigating the brooding mesa-like backdrops in *Raiders of the Lost Ark*. Past the apocalyptic earth craters and machinery, there was this nice stretch of pinelands that led down to the shore. I once stumbled upon a spot where the ground made a bowl in the earth and the water was trapped. There, among the sturdy stalks of fluted thrush, the soft hints of pink orchids, I discovered an entire colony of egrets. Skimming the surface of the black water, their wings swelled like reams of rice paper.

It caused me to wonder if it were possible that Dad and Sebastian were still with Leonora Marino and me. Watching those egrets snowflaking the water and trees, I wondered if Dad hadn't turned into that meadow of sadly beautiful trees creaking in the breeze, while Sebastian took on the form of that unassuming, one-eyed cat whose path I kept crossing.

Chapter Fifteen

After supper, we lounged around feeling too full to play charades or do much more than be stationary. Vivian had already excused herself. She had a headache, she said, and so my mother suggested she take a lie-down, Vivian could use her room.

Mythic Ethel arrived while I was slumped on the couch, pretending to read while Aunt Ginny wound Charlize's hair in curlers. A man she called her butler had driven her, although this butler was, from what we understood, really just a generous neighbor Uncle Tuck paid for the trouble Mythic Ethel caused him. From Horatio's neck hung a large silver cross crusted with gemstones; I wondered if the cross was normally part of Horatio's ensemble, or if it were an addition to appease Mythic Ethel.

Feeling too sluggish to do much more than take a stab at politeness—when really, all I wanted to do was close the door to my room, hole up with my mother's dolls, and never come out—I listened from the couch as my mother asked Horatio if he wanted something to eat. "Or sangria. Please join us for sangria. I made it myself."

The sangria of which my mother was speaking was Franzia to which she'd added canned peaches.

Before Horatio could even venture a reply, Mythic Ethel protested with a, "No, no, no, Leo. Hore, here, has to get back home."

"It's Leonora, Aunt Ethel."

"I know that, Leonardo, I do. Now listen, Hore already got us lost on the way because of that idiotic machine. I told you before we started out that we oughtn't rely on that Tom-Tom to get us where we needed to be—didn't I, Hore? Dreadful woman, that Tom-Tom, let me tell you."

As Uncle Tuck lugged Mythic Ethel's trunk and inexplicable hatbox in from Horatio's car, Mythic Ethel came shuffling into the living room, prodding a cardboard box forward with the feet of her walker.

"Hold your horses there, Sisyphus," Uncle Tuck called, swooping Mythic Ethel's ratty box under his arm and using his free hand to guide her. "Eva's looking lonely over there. Why don't you go and have a seat next to her? Can I get you anything? A sweetie from the kitchen?"

"I can get a sweetie from the kitchen just fine on my own."

Mythic Ethel was as delighted to oppose you as she was to avail the knowledge she alone had the experience and wherewithal to dispose. At that moment, she was moving her mouth around a lot, the tip of her tongue spasmodically nipping out. She resembled a toad whose deep green maw you expected a fly to dart out of.

"Now, I'm very tired from the long journey and need to sit down. So long, Hore. Thanks for the adventure." Mythic Ethel waved lavishly without looking at Horatio, who made a little bow before shuffling awkwardly out of the door. I had the impression he was as in a hurry to hightail it out of my mother's bridal shower as Mythic Ethel was to get rid of her butler. Clearly, he was crimping her style.

I could feel Mythic Ethel's cushiony girth as she lowered herself beside me, the couch springs groaning under her weight. Holy thunderbird, did she smell like hamburger!

Grunting her "hello, hello's," unable to muster the energy to do more than grunt and nod at us each in turn, Mythic Ethel turned her head at a rather preternatural angle to demand that Charlize "Come over and take a seat in front of me, that's right! You'd be the spitting image of Shirley Temple if your mother had the foresight to give you curlers," she shot a disparaging look at Vivian, who was gathering her slacks in her fists, primed for a fight. I had the startling thought of an incensed cat pawing at a very immobile toad—an image that prompted a bad taste in my mouth.

Charlize stared like Mythic Ethel was some kind of stuffed creature plopped behind a pane of glass. "Mommy didn't do it," she pointed at my aunt. "Grandma Ginny did."

Mythic Ethel nudged the box toward Charlize. Filled with rubber doll babies and old model cars, the box had subsisted for so long in her garage, it smelled like firewood and dead birds. It was also the key to what Mythic Ethel deemed her greatest offering: every broken, moldy toy inside it offered a means for her to bait innocents into sitting through her Christian teachings.

As Charlize became acquainted with a stuffed pelican bearing a mysterious brown blot on its belly, Mythic Ethel began telling the story of Jesus and the Leper. Five minutes into the story, when she got to the part about the healing—she really drew things out—I'm pretty sure Mythic Ethel let one loose. I could feel it happen in the cushions.

Chapter Sixteen

It was the summer I turned fifteen when, upon returning from my freshman year at Moore Hedge, where literally every peer was a shithead, things began to really change.

My folks had sent me to Moore Hedge Academy for "a good education." A cover-up for the real reason, which was for me to get over Sebastian. Also, maybe my parents were trying to patch things up while I was gone? Hard to say now. Because at that point, Finn and Sebastian had moved across the country after Dad and my mother had already spent my childhood pretending to be a real couple.

Other than Justina and Daria and the rest of the motel crew, I was a loner without Sebastian; nothing felt stable at Moore Hedge but the compulsory calf-length kilt, whose indestructibleness made it even more hideous. I'd actually named the thing "Kit" and attached it to a pole, which I waved around the bungalow during my first summer home, hoping to spur a rebellion. I wasn't sure what I was trying to prove, other than my extreme discontent with the injustice of our class.

When the hired driver who'd ferried me from the airport pulled up to our driveway, I'd felt invested with the authority of Yahweh, whose miracles we'd been learning about in Moore Hedge's mandatory Bible study.

"Let my peeps go!" I exclaimed the moment my mother appeared on the porch, Caboodle writhing in her arms. Apparently, my mother had acquired her poufy-assed Shih Tzu to fill in the nest my spot at Moore Hedge had made vacant. To round off Caboodle's snaggle tooth, which protruded from his frosty white beard, Caboodle was obviously a lodestone for fleas; he was scratching himself with his hind legs in a most caustic manner.

I can remember the intensity of feeling I'd harbored as I walked toward my parents. My mother, wrangling that snipping snowball while my Dad joined her on the porch.

What I had wanted to do more than anything in that moment was dive back into the car. Turn my back on my Dad's flushed face, my mother puppetting Caboodle's paw in a wave.

Roll up the tinted hired car's window and tell the driver he'd dropped me off at the wrong house—I'd never seen those people before. "Please take me anywhere else."

I'd already gotten nowhere with my mother when I asked if I could please take on a job as one of the motel maids in exchange for staying home. I hated school more than she knew.

"Why do you hate it so much?" Dad asked flatly.

Ever since I got back, it was like Dad was physically inflated and emotionally drained. Like the verve had been suction-cupped out of him and replaced by a flushed complexion. His face became wider, his jowls pink and slackened. While he had gotten physically broader, his personality had compensated by getting smaller. What I mean is, he seemed to be constantly brooding and silent. I didn't like it.

"Eva?" My mother leaned forward. "Answer your father," she said. Though without the severity one might align with a daughter's mother allying with this same daughter's father. We were sitting at the dining room table, in the same places we'd assumed the summer we got back from camp and my parents had told me Finn and Sebastian were leaving—Dad at the head of the table, facing the wall displaying the products of my mother's quilting phase, my mother across the heirloom mirror with the cracks spiderwebbing the center.

I faced the window that looked out to the same sea, shelving foam and veined with green.

"I don't have any friends." I looked at Dad. "I'd rather stay here. I can work for you, Dad. I can clean the motels just as well as

Justina and Daria, you know—they'll show me the ropes, I'll make myself useful. Did you know none of the girls at Moore Hedge like to read books?" I shot a meaningful glance at my mother. "All they do is talk about boys and "What is a clitoris?" and SparkNote the shit out of *Huck Finn*. And Sister Thomasina scares the fuck out—"

"Watch your language, young lady."

"You sound like Sister Thomasina," I said. "Try learning the Pythagorean theorem with her as your teacher and you wouldn't want to study geometry, either."

"Listen, Eva," my mother intervened again. Pulling at the academy's compulsory kilt I'd worn home in protest, I thought the sorry sight of me in it might convey a fraction of just how unhappy I was. "Honey, that's probably why the Moore Hedge girls are making fun of you. You look like Laura Ingalls Wilder. Maybe if we just altered—"

"Eva looks very nice," Dad said to the wall of quilts. "I don't know who Laura Ingalls Wilder is, but that sure as hell better be a compliment, Leonora."

"Watch your language, mister." I held up a finger.

Dad speared a hunk of food, studied it thoughtfully, and said, "You two. Always ganging up on me."

It is only recently that I have begun to consider how hard it must have been for Dad to live with me and my mother.

The day after I challenged Dad, he sat me down with Mandy, a girl several years my senior, who'd dropped out of the Ship Bottom public school system when she discovered she was pregnant.

Mandy had joined Dad's staff just after Christmas, when Daria set her to work closing The Pugnacious Pirate down for the season. The Pugnacious Pirate had always been the least popular of the motels, and when business was slow, Dad said it was better to hole it up for the winter—no one wants to spend Christmas in a room adorned with skulls and crossbones.

Upon Mandy's arrival, Dad promptly marshaled us to the patio table, on which he'd arranged boxed cookies and juice pouches. I'm not sure what mystified me more, that Dad had taken the time to prepare the table, or that he thought a tray of Lorna Doones would break the ice between me and Mandy. She was as different from me as could be. In the galaxy of celestial energy, I was Uranus to Mandy's Jupiter. Or Pluto, which may not even be a planet.

"Take this job away from me, Eva, and I swear . . ." Mandy warned.

I waved my hands, correcting Mandy before she could get further confused.

"I'm not trying to take anything away from you. I want to have one of—"

"Whatever you do, you just can't leave school." Mandy twirled the end of her braid, which was dyed the color of pink lemonade. "Dropping out isn't cool."

Dropping out isn't cool, I mused, and reached for a Hi-C. Mandy's hair was making me thirsty.

"Did my dad put you up to this?" I asked.

Mandy tapped her front tooth with her nail. A gesture that seemed demonstrative of a mean girl.

"I'll give you a dollar if you confess," I pressed.

"Your dad already gave me twenty." Examining the fan of cookies, Mandy crammed several into each of her bra cups and shrugged. "Can I have my dollar now?"

That same summer, I secured an internship with the local paper to occupy the months I spent in Ship Bottom without Sebastian. The position was all thanks to Dad's plan to better me, first, at Moore Hedge Academy, then, with some real-world experience. He seemed to want me to do anything that kept my mother apart from me.

Now I understand that my withdrawal from my home life—my refusal to even try to find a beacon among Moore Hedge's Academy of Assholes—as well as the anger that had been planted at the whiplash of Sebastian's leave-taking, helped lay the foundation of my depression.

My mother's approach to my receding from everything was much different. "C'mon, get up, let's go shopping!" she'd say on my days off from interning with the paper. Which were also the days my mother was likely to catch me doing something along the lines of compulsively plaiting my hair into tiny snake braids—something I did after another letter I'd sent to Sebastian went unacknowledged. When I look back on my high school summers in Ship Bottom, I remember first the interminable waiting, the anticipation of that which even I could not define.

At *The Ship Bottom Herald*, my main responsibilities included making sure the printer had enough ink and paper and emptying the trash bins. When I got to tag along for a story—usually an arts feature like Ship Bottom's annual Puppy Bowl, Kite-a-Thon, or Cake Bake-Off—I ended up toting sunscreen, VIP passes, voice recorders, and bottled water in the manner of a country club golf caddy, minus the cool bag and penchant for offering unsolicited moral support. Sometimes—say, if the reporter whom I was shadowing was immersed in an interview with the previous year's hot-dog-eating champion—I'd take out my memo pad to pen copious notes. Investing less attention in what I was writing than in the volume of whatever bull I could scribble, all while biting my bottom lip to assimilate the utmost degree of professionalism.

I think I still might do this—bite my lip in a thoughtful way—when I try to record for Shiloh just exactly what I'm trying to say.

"Write your story down, Eva," she'd said. "It doesn't matter if it doesn't have a perfect beginning and end."

But the story about Sebastian and me did have a clear beginning and end: *Once upon a time, we were children. And then, Sebastian was dead while I went on playing pretend.*

"Remember, Eva, that whatever you decide to write doesn't just have to be about Sebastian," Shiloh said.

"I know," I told her.

To complete his efforts to "better me," Dad also wanted me to have a "normal" summer job. "Your mother never had one of those," he said, as if my mother's lack of work experience were a qualifier for mine.

And so the summer before I graduated from Moore Hedge Academy, I got a gig at The Fudge Kitchen on Main Street.

The worst part of the job was also the best: I was required to wear matchstick pants, a cellophane chef's hat, and plastic gloves while offering tourists samples of our fudge. I'd stand under the blistering sun and deliver the cubed samples into waiting palms. The problem was that so much fudge was wasted—because it was so hot out, I'd have to go back inside and swap the puddled cubes out for fresh ones. But whatever. The perk of the position was that it was kind of like giving Holy Communion. Except by the end of my shifts, my hands smelled like rubber on account of the disposable gloves required to distribute the fudge.

Chapter Seventeen

Charlize's one rescue from Mythic Ethel's box was Music Baby, a doll named for the tune that played when you wound the notch protruding from her cloth bottom. The melody was somber—a cross between "Mary Had a Little Lamb" and "Twinkle, Twinkle Little Star." But even that didn't seem to matter anymore, because Music Baby had been through so much, you could hardly decipher the tune that came out of her.

I already thought of the doll as a joke, on account of the bush of yellow hair that sprang from her scalp. Then, to disguise the magic marker Vivian and I had colored the doll's face with as children, my mother tried repainting Music Baby's rubber head a bluish gray that by no means blended into the original shade. And so, between her painted face and preternatural quantity of hair, Music Baby was frightening to behold. Therefore, I was reasonably sure Charlize was the only seven-year-old in the world to see past the horror that was Music Baby and love the doll anyway.

For the rest of the evening, Charlize carried the doll around with her, holding her in her lap during charades and afterwards, setting her on the step stool my mother obligingly placed alongside Charlize during dessert.

Before bed, I found Charlize in her Scooby Doo jammies and slippers, brushing her teeth in front of the bathroom mirror. Music Baby was propped against a tub of lotion.

"Hey, kiddo."

Charlize turned the faucet on, spit, then filled a Dixie cup with water, which she swished around in her mouth, blinking wide-eyed at her reflection. She spit the water out in a neat little puddle.

"Hello," she answered with the primness of the president of a women's gardening society. That was it. I was convinced Charlize was an eighty-year-old lady transplanted into a first grader's body.

I nodded at Music Baby. "I see you've got a new friend. I used to play with her a lot when I was your age."

Charlize looked at me, disturbed and impressed by my capacity to talk and brush my teeth at the same time. "Her name's Cabbage," she said.

"Cabbage?"

"Yeah. She keeps crying," Charlize added sagely.

I hawked out my toothpaste in one thick clot. "That's because she can play music through her butt."

"What?"

I wiped my mouth on the back of my wrist and levelled myself with Charlize. "I hear you're staying in my room."

"Yeah." Charlize turned her face purposely away from me. "Mommy said she needs to keep her eyes on Great Aunt Ef-fel."

"Do you have a bed for Cabbage?"

"A what?"

Charlize followed me into my old room, where from the back of my closet, I dug out the wooden doll cradle Dad brought back for me after one of his travels. "There. How's that?"

Charlize frowned. "It's small."

"I'm sure Cabbage will be able to manage. You ready for bed?"

Nodding and kicking off her puppy dog slippers, Charlize pressed Music Baby into the cradle, then climbed onto the futon, and—lying on her stomach with her arms and legs splayed out like a starfish, her ponytail matted down her spine—was asleep in minutes.

As I listened to Charlize's breathing, I thought about the time Sebastian and I snuck into The Mystic Mermaid. I remembered vividly the smell of the room, boarded up for the winter. The feeling of skin on a stiff mattress. The press of the dark. What we had done after . . .

I quickly fell into the trap of replaying the memory while, on the futon below, Charlize began mumbling in her sleep, making sucking sounds with her mouth, which didn't help.

I reached for my phone, and using the light from its screen, skimmed the titles of the spines of my mother's self-help books on my nightstand. No doubt she'd left them for me to find. My mother was not afraid to be direct when it came to dropping hints. Little did she know how many self-help books I'd combed on my own.

I selected the one called *The Pillars of Happiness: Expanded Edition!* Then I wondered if "expanded" meant that the author, a Mr. Harold Smuthers, had gone so far as to add an extra pillar.

Before I knew it, it was morning.

Chapter Eighteen

It wasn't until some time after Dad passed that I fully realized he must've known what was going on between Finn and my mother. I mean, how could he not have? Growing up, Finn was always coming by for something or other, and whenever my mother invited Sebastian and him over for dinner, she'd act as though including Finn was only an afterthought: "He doesn't have anyone to cook for him," she'd add when she mentioned our guests to Dad. Never mind that when it was just me and my mother, Finn was the one to cook Sebastian and us supper—even when they were the ones who came over.

In Leonora Marino's version of the story behind Ship Bottom's enigmatic bachelor and his son, Sebastian's mother walked out on her partner and infant son.

When my mother first told me this story, the idea conjured the image of a faceless woman stepping, ghost-like, through the father of my best friend. Which was why I never asked Sebastian his side of the story. Because I believed my mother, and her version of the story was too sad to be repeated.

After Sebastian died, Finn vanished from our lives. My mother just about went crazy when he didn't return her calls—I'd never seen her that way, and can objectively say she was far worse than I had been, during those years at Moore Hedge Academy when Sebastian failed to write back to me. Where I stomped around the house or withdrew to my frilly pink room on the summers I was home, my mother passed her time drinking. Sometimes, she smashed things, leaving the vacuum and broom dangerously blocked with shards. She dropped fifteen pounds in a matter of weeks, and my mother was already petite to begin with. The change was not an attractive one.

It had all happened so fast: first, Finn and Sebastian reappearing, Odysseus and Telemachus back from some impromptu father-son journey, having caught wind of Dad dying; then Finn disappearing immediately after we said our final goodbyes to no-longer-living Sebastian.

At that point, my dwelling on what Sebastian was doing in the years his father and he were away ended abruptly. I stopped picturing Sebastian kissing other women, Finn slipping into the homes of others who were not my mother. Instead, lying awake at night, I'd replay the last time I saw Sebastian.

My memory of that day was like a magic trick. One moment, Sebastian was there, and the next, he was gone. *Drowned*, I reminded myself. And unlike the first time he moved away, back when Dad and Sebastian were both still living, it was clear that this time the chance of Finn returning seemed far from likely. Finn and Sebastian were a two-for-one, after all. I realized that only after the fact, which is to say, now. Altogether, the four of us were too similar; Finn and Sebastian were as entangled as Leonora Marino and me. Without Sebastian, Finn was as gone as his son. Had I been the one to jump from the rocks and drown in the gorge, I do not doubt that my mother would have disappeared, as well.

So it was that everything my mother and I understood to be safe became untenable. Left quaking with longing, we tethered ourselves to each other. After Leonora Marino and I lost Dad, I thought she and I could never be closer. But the death of a loved one draws those the dead leave behind together. Just at the juncture where I thought it would be impossible for the bond I had with my mother to grow stronger, the love we had for each other proved my presumption wrong. It was almost painful, our closeness, no matter how different we were. Like our differences had congealed into one unit, there existed no words to explain us.

The sensation that I was pedaling back in time, shedding whatever advancements I'd made in my profession—not to mention, as a person—fell by the wayside: no more impressive writing job for me at *Eat Right!* For now, anyway, or ever, I was beginning to think.

By now I could not imagine myself tromping back into the office in my spool heels, assuming my desk with the glamor I'd inherited as the magazine's kale expert. It seemed incredible that there was a period when I'd pull together an outfit whose conception was derivative of sheer laziness, and my colleagues at *Eat Right!* would throw a fit, they'd just adore it. One day I'd worn a night shirt as a baby doll dress, and when the art director asked what was the meaning of this—"You look fucking fantastic!"—I told Troy the meaning was that I was conjuring my inner Mia Farrow: "You know, the one in *Rosemary's Baby*."

By the by, I measured the months that followed Sebastian's death by observing my neighbors, the habits of strangers. How, specifically, they marked the year's passing by decorating their personal and business properties.

Halloween brought out the inflatable boogies. Then a powdering of white puff paint reminiscent of snow replaced the cornucopia window clings. Wreathes hung on storefront doors, some garlanded with mistletoe or chains of tinsel. Then came the season of Christmas, whose ho-ho-hoing seemed to go on the longest. Exhausted by the festivities of secret Santa, champagne toasts, and poppers from which burst paper crowns and useless objects to add to the detritus, many of my neighbors became lazy, the thrill of New Year's resolutions quickly receding into an indolence that brought their vigor down a peg. Those I had come upon attempting trends such as Nordic walking and bullet coffee—lost their luster. And the newbies I had encountered swishing through the freezing sea air in their brand-new neoprene jerkins and Sketchers sloghed Ship Bottom in their puffers, plodding the old snow like befuddled zombies.

The Christmas trees lined the curb at my complex into February, when the puff paint crusting the windows mocked the mud-streaked banks of snow holding steadfast to the sides of the road. Middle-aged men partaking in the ten-dollar bouquets and googly-eyed stuffed animal specials lined CVS pharmacy when, exceptionally blue, I made a trip specifically to purchase one of the heart-shaped boxes of chocolates for myself. I devoured the box on the icy cold trudge back to my apartment, then tore the bow from the lid and stuck it in my hair. An hour later, I was retching. It was the raspberry cream ones that did it. Being lactose intolerant, I probably shouldn't have finished all of the chocolates. The long and short of it is, my one attempt at festiveness went to shit and even the bow that went to the top of the lid ended up in the toilet.

Trying my best to keep busy and sane, by the time late winter turned into spring, I'd invented every possible outcome that could have brought a different end for Sebastian. Sometimes, I'd imagine being in the car with him, a truck spinning out in front of us on the highway—the driver having fallen asleep at the wheel at the same moment we were cruising at seventy-five miles-per-hour, straight for his cargo.

Then, in my fabulating, the passage into death unfurled as gently as a G-rated movie. There was Sebastian looking over at me, half-smiling in his confusion because he knew death was upon him, he knew we would part as the truck and our car made contact at just the right moment and amount of speed for our bodies to flunk forward.

I let this rendering of Sebastian's death slip into a cartoon. One with painted blue jays tweeting in circles around my head while Sebastian sat motionless but slightly smiling beside me. And even when he didn't speak—even when I knew he'd said his farewell just by gazing contentedly at me—when I reached out to touch my best friend once more, his hand was still warm.

Chapter Nineteen

At breakfast, Uncle Tuck, donning his shearling-lined bathrobe, was the bearer of good news: a traveling carnival had sprung up in an abandoned parking lot at the center of Ship Bottom. Would we all like to go?

And so that night, all of us but Mythic Ethel, whose bedtime was promptly after supper—"I need at least thirteen hours of sleep in order to function, goslings"—went to the carnival. Uncle Tuck and Aunt Ginny even relinquished their ponchos for normal-looking clothes, and Charlize put on a pair of orange plaid overalls that almost made her look like a normal little girl. Leonora Marino wore a banner that said "Bride-to-Be" crossing her shoulder, and having dropped Mythic Ethel back at the hotel, Vivian arrived looking like she was going to attend a middle-aged woman's knitting club from the 80s in her crocheted sweater, side ponytail, and stonewashed jeggings.

Uncle Tuck won Aunt Ginny a massive stuffed bull by tossing a hula-hoop around a crate, then treated us all to chicken-on-a-stick and cherry colas. "We can skip the Silicon Valley diet for one day, can't we, honey?" he shouted over the stuffed bull obscuring Aunt Ginny from view. Later, after we watched a monster truck show-down during which Vivian shouted that her head was going to split open, we decided we'd take one more ride and head home. My mother traipsed off with Uncle Tuck and Aunt Ginny for one last spin on the Tilt-A-Whirl, leaving Vivian, Charlize, and me to wander the park on our own.

"Anything else you want to do?" Vivian asked her daughter.

Charlize was picking at her bag of cotton candy, Music Baby's head poking out from her backpack, on which was printed a bewildering combination of pink-frosted cupcakes and galloping ponies. Her lips were ringed blue and her face was smudged in dust like she'd ducked away when nobody was looking to eat her cotton candy.

I suggested we take a tour through the funhouse.

"The Barrel of Monkeys?" Vivian shot me a look. "That'll frighten Charlize, that place even scares the pants off me."

You're wearing jeggings! I wanted to shout.

Instead, I balled my hands into fists. "What about the dragon coaster?"

Vivian paused to consider.

"Mommy!" Charlize said loudly, her face turned skyward.

"What is it, honey?"

Charlize was pointing. "Look at the clouds."

"It does look like a storm, doesn't it?" my cousin cooed down at her daughter. "We should probably just dash after my parents, Eva. Find your mom, and—"

"Alright!" I clapped my hands together and wheeled on my heel. "I'll go on my own. See you two back at the car."

"Eva. Eva, wait—"

"Where's she going?" I heard Charlize ask. But I had already turned my back.

Emboldened by the carnival lanterns, the smattering of stars, I headed into the lights—

Too late, Vivian.

The man who took my ticket at The Barrel of Monkeys was so frail, he looked like a cardboard cutout that could easily tip over.

"All by yourself?"

I nodded. The man's clothes smelled like tobacco and cinnamon toast. I wanted to hug him until I noticed the tattoo of a fat pink breast on his forearm. Or was that a donut?

"Know your way around?" he called.

I walked straight through the turnstile and into the dark. It took a minute for me to catch my bearings, allow my eyes to adjust. There were distorted mirrors on the walls, in every direction my reflection stretched out or else turned into itself, made squat and neckless.

I kept bumping into the walls. I'd do a 180 and there I was. Another turn of the head, and there was another Eva staring dumbly back. Then, I'd hear a child laughing or crying out from somewhere ahead or behind, but by the time I was near it, the voice was an echo coming from several directions. I eventually came upon a large room with an old carousel horse at its center. The horse was dust-coated when I ran a finger across its grimy, jewel-crusted saddle. I was grateful there were no longer any mirrors, just unfinished wood walls reeking of something that smelled like shoe polish.

I made my way through a narrow tunnel that brought me to the gigantic revolving barrel. A trio of children were trying to scramble their way up its side before tumbling. They were too occupied to notice me traveling the thin walkway adjacent to the barrel. Reaching the other side and climbing a short ladder, I wobbled to cross a bridge. Constructed of spools that shifted underfoot, the bridge made a sound like pins knocking in an old bowling alley. It was upon reaching the end that I found the woman lying at the bottom of the walkway.

The woman twitched with her whole body, as if she were trying to breathe, but couldn't. Clusters of seashells adorned her hair, silver-green scales glinted on her willowy skirt. Was the woman part of a performance? An actress, perhaps, from the carnival's troupe? There were people paid to dress up as princes and witches, court jesters and queens. Perhaps she was even drunk and had just wandered into The Barrel of Monkeys for kicks, before she got sick.

There is something to be said about going with your gut. About doing whatever your instincts tell you to do, before reality catches up and outshines that impulse. I couldn't tell whether the woman was crying or not, or if she was, in fact, as ill as I thought, but I could hear footsteps clacking through the passage, the children's voices rising up the ladder. I took a step closer and reached out my hand, and then the woman turned around, and it was as if every mirror in the funhouse crashed down. The creaking and groaning of the rotating barrel roared in my ears, and I ran. I ran and I ran.

~~~

When Aunt Ginny found me standing in the wet field where the last of the cars were parked, shivering all over as the rain pelted down, she shed her t-shirt and slung it over my shoulders. In the distance, the wind was thrashing the tops of the motionless rides and howling off the tin roof of the gazebo. The tents for the concession stands popped inside and out, like umbrella tops, while Aunt Ginny held me by the shoulders. Wild-eyed as she explained that she, Uncle Tuck, and my mother had all split up to go looking for me. Vivian and Charlize had even gone off to see if I was still in The Barrel of Monkeys. Even after Aunt Ginny shook me gently by the shoulders, asking anxiously, "What in heaven's name is the matter with you, Eva? Tell Ginny!" my throat was swollen and raw, and I could find no voice to speak with at all.
~~~

Chapter Twenty

How did Sebastian die?

I wish I could say anything but the truth of it all—I imagine it's never easy explaining anything behind death, although I felt it was easier to blame it on someone, or on something else entirely.

When a bad heart took Dad, I blamed science, the environment, Dad's genetics. I blamed the doctors for not catching Dad's symptoms sooner, even though Dad refused to step foot inside a doctor's office until my mother threatened to leave him.

But he couldn't have been helped sooner. I knew that, I did. The diagnosis was easy because by the time Dad went in to be checked, it was already too late. He was so dizzy he couldn't keep his food down. Also, I think he had given up on living. In the end, he didn't even try to stop me from calling emergency.

"So, how did Sebastian die?" Shiloh asked me months after my skirting the question I knew she already had the answer to.

Just to come out with it, to lay it all on the table, was like turning something sharp around in my chest with my own hand.

"Well, even more unexpectedly than Dad's heart attack claimed Dad—"

That, I believe, is what I finally told Shiloh.

As kids, Sebastian and I had nearly lost our lives jumping into the gorge below the steep, craggy rocks between our houses. I can still remember the bite of the brine in my throat, the bitterness stinging my nostrils, as having already committed to the fantasy and jumped we were mowed down by the water.

No. Part of the water. For, finally, there was something that felt much stronger than us. And as my best friend's and my handhold broke and the cold filled my lungs, I wondered if this would be the last time I saw Sebastian.

It wasn't, of course. Because even when I could not determine up from down, when I flailed my arms—trying to buoy myself up to the top—it was Sebastian who seized me by the waist and swam me to the surface. It was Sebastian who saved us, and broke us. Because he was the one who left and because he was the one who wanted to go back to the rocks after he finally came back. And we did—we did go back to the rocks. And once back, it was as if we had never left.

But this time it's going to be different, Sebastian assured me last spring. We were older and stronger the day he suggested we try it again together—*It's been years, Eva!*

And I hadn't agreed to Sebastian's dare to jump in with him. I'd been afraid of the current and told him.

Please? Sebastian pushed his fingers through my hair.

Standing on the edge of the bluff, I looked down at Sebastian's bare feet and kicked off my sandals. Felt the rough grit of the rocks underfoot.

Be a kid with me again? he pleaded. *For old time's sake, Eva?* He reached for my hand.

You sound like an old man, I'd laughed. Trying to make a joke of the moment. There was no way he could be serious. We were young and stupid when we'd jumped, and we were lucky we'd survived. But then I can remember Sebastian's expression upon turning to face him. The excitement and the awful terror of it. And then I wrangled my hand from his.

I ran away after it happened. I was delirious, I was jamming the rewind button back on time.

Nothing made sense as I sprinted to Finn's. And then, bursting into his house, I yanked my mother and him wildly apart. Finn, who had been on top of my mother. My mother, who was all surprise and smudged lipstick. A girl caught in the back of a car with a boy.

I felt as if I were screaming, tearing out my lungs for someone to do something, do something, now! Then there was an ambulance, police cars. Because eventually, I must have said something. Or Finn or my mother must have realized when they asked, "Where is Sebastian?"

The rescue divers brought up a body they said had been lodged between two boulders and the trunk of a fallen tree. Sebastian's body which was no longer his body, but an imitation of one. Too cold and unchanging to be convincing enough.

Of course, I didn't see the body then. This is only what I imagined in the time it took me to try to forget what happened and to begin to forgive.

My memories of the moments I breathlessly ran into Finn's was a wash, a brown out. There was Finn throwing my mother off him. There was Finn's cordless slipping from my mother's shaking hands, the battery popping out of the end.

Someone knocked a tall glass of water from the island over and it shattered. No. I threw a tall glass of vodka and seltzer off the island and it shattered.

There was an officer flashing his badge, the badge so shiny it blinded me. The officer dangling a pair of sandals in front of my face, telling me these were found on the rocks, are they yours?

When a second officer came to question me, I was sitting with my knees to my chest on my mother's couch, shivering as he asked me, "Did you notice anything different about your friend's behavior that seemed off? Had your friend been under the influence? Did he fall in the gorge, or did he jump?"

I was unable to do anything but shake my head again and again, until eventually my mother got fed up with watching the interrogation and told him that was enough, it's time for you to go now. "Officers, my daughter has been through enough. I'm asking you to get out of my house."

If I had listened to my gut and refused to accompany Sebastian on the rocks. If I had convinced him to stay. *Let's hang back with Finn and my mother, let's all just keep drinking vodka seltzers!* If I hadn't agreed to go with him, then all the others who'd flooded my mother's and my lives would recede into the backdrop, go the way of my mother's and my grief. A grief felt all the deeper because we were still getting over Dad, whose death also felt like a trick.

All the while, I wouldn't talk to anyone, it was like my mouth was filled with cotton. My mother would ask me to please just talk to her—"Eva, will you please say something, darling"—and all I could do was turn from her, look out the window. Sometimes I even shut my eyes right in front of her, while she was still talking. And I did not just do this in front of her, I did it at the office and the grocery store, too. I did it without realizing, because even on the inside of my eyelids, what I saw over and again was Sebastian standing beside me between his old cottage and ours. One moment on the edge of the rocks, and the next, stepping off.

I can still see the sea crashing below us. The waves, white and thick as whipped topping. The arrow Sebastian's body made in the air. I can still hear the crush of the water as he shot toward the frothing mouth of the gorge and the waves opened to receive him.

The scene replayed like a broken tape of which there existed only one copy. Because I had been the only one with Sebastian, the only one to see it happen.

When you become used to being surrounded by something magical, that which is magical becomes natural. And because Sebastian and I grew up along the coast of Ship Bottom, we believed ourselves to be invincible to its dangers. Death by drowning was an impossibility for Sebastian and me. We'd grown up by the sea.

After weeks of avoiding Shiloh's questions—passing the hour bowing my head—I eventually brought up Sebastian on my own.

"He's dead," I blurted.

I hadn't been listening to what Shiloh was saying. I hadn't heard what she'd asked me. All I'd seen was her mouth moving, when over the static, I'd laid it all out: "He's dead and it's all my fault."

After my confession, Shiloh told me that finding an outlet to talk about what had happened was crucial to moving forward. That forming a narrative would help me cope, and that it was okay if the memories didn't line up. It was okay if I was talking in circles or that what I was saying was out of sequence. "That's how thoughts work."

Now, do you see that talking about what happened is what I'm trying to do? I am trying to recover. I want to move forward. I blame myself for Sebastian's death. And from there, the loss of my happiness. My mother's and my happiness.

Chapter Twenty-one

The morning after the carnival, I awoke to Caboodle humping my shoulder and the room bathed in light. From downstairs, I could hear the television and some clanking around in the kitchen. Charlize was already up and out, the futon made, the cradle for Music Baby empty.

I shuffled down the hall and into the bathroom, only to find myself face-to-face with Uncle Tuck. To my horror, he was sitting on the pot, reading the paper.

"Good morning!" he chimed, toasting the air with my mother's beloved "No One Shits on My Shih Tzu" mug.

Whatever I needed to do in the bathroom was no longer important. I would hold my bladder all weekend if need be. Who cared if my hair was combed, my teeth brushed? The faster I forgot the sight of Uncle Tuck doing his business with the jollity of a local perching on the counter at The Happy Clam Diner, the better. I'd forgo any hygiene routine to cleanse my mind of what I'd seen—Uncle Tuck doing what he did best, which meant embarrassing the women in his life at every chance.

In the kitchen, Aunt Ginny was sticking bright yellow Peeps around the top of a frosted cake. Meanwhile, on the television, some nut on HGTV was trying to renovate a cabin that looked like the watery site where the Pied Piper lured legions of rats to die.

"Toots on a string!" she yelped when she saw me in the doorway. There was way too much bodily-related imagery being offered that morning, and I hadn't even had my coffee. The sight of the high-test brew burbling happily from my mother's Moccamaster recalled the sight of Uncle Tuck doing the do, my mother's puppy mug in hand.

"You scared me!" Aunt Ginny wagged her spatula. Wearing an insulated yellow poncho, she looked like the Big Bird of Peeps. "I didn't think anyone but Tuck was around."

"Oh, he's around all right," I said. Ignoring the mirror behind Aunt Ginny's head—in the brief glimpse I caught, I saw a person with the wild-haired, stony-faced semblance of Medusa. *Top of the morning to you, Eva Marino!*

I nabbed a mug and one of the Peeps and examined Aunt Ginny's creation. I could see what she was going for with the round chocolate cake ringed with the yellow marshmallow birds. She had attempted some sort of artistic expression with the spatula that just made it messy. The cake was supposed to look like a sunflower, but something about the Peeps gave it a menacing feel, what with them all peering into the center.

I poured myself a cup of coffee, bit the head off the Peep and chewed. God, I had forgotten how awful Peeps were.

Aunt Ginny must have seen the shift in my expression, because she was already exclaiming, "What's wrong? No one likes Peeps, do they? I *knew* I should have steered clear from *Real Simple*! 'Real simple' my ass," she glowered at the chocolate and Peep mound.

"Things could be worse." I nodded at the television. The cabin renovations underway, the guy on HGTV was now gutting a reservoir in which the desiccated carcass of an alligator had been discovered.

The official shower festivities began once everyone gathered back at the house, by which time I'd been able to change out of my pajamas and help out. Assisting Aunt Ginny in the doctoring of the Peep cake wasn't made easier by Aunt Ginny's poncho. I kept suggesting she take it off while we decorated—"Aunt Ginny, your neoprene's getting in the frosting!"—but she was too busy blaming the recipe to consider giving up her sweat-boosting apparel.

In the end, I didn't think the cake looked half bad, but Aunt Ginny was still teary because though the final result was fifty shades better than the one I'd come downstairs to, the marshmallow birds were still not situated in a perfect ring, like the picture in the magazine.

To get the party started, my mother suggested games like "Bridal Bingo" and "Sweetheart Pictionary," a two-player competition that involved designing a wedding dress out of toilet paper. Nobody wanted to play, so we forgot about those games and played charades like we would normally do. Charades was one of the few occasions that necessitated my mother and her brother mime their actions rather than perform them at volume. When my mother had acted in her living room performances with Finn when Sebastian and I were kids, the fluidity with which she'd slipped into character was made more dramatic by how far her voice carried. Even when she hadn't put herself into a Shakespearean character, my mother was loud enough by nature to elicit the attention of all God's living creatures. The same went for her brother, who had the most trouble keeping his mouth shut while he was in charge of cluing us into his charade. His silent representation of *To Kill a Mockingbird* was terrifying not only because of the passion of his arm-flapping, but because while drawing his hand across his throat to indicate slashing, a terrible noise emerged from his throat. The sound was something between a crow and a burp.

Gift time, and my mother was the lucky recipient of some risque lingerie—Mythic Ethel wasn't a fan—from Aunt Ginny and a sachet of essential oils Mythic Ethel said were to be used only when my mother was praying.

"Otherwise, it's witchcraft, Leonardo." My mother was having far too good a time to remind her that her name was "Leonora."

Vivian and Charlize presented my mother with some variety of fern that stunk. It must have been sprayed in fox urine to divert vermin, but because Vivian had tied a bow around the pot to make the fern look festive and whatnot, I'm pretty sure everyone pretended her offering didn't smell like a cheeseball rolled in garlic and socks.

Overall, everything was going great, and I was happy that my mother had pulled this off herself. What a dud of a Maid of Honor I was! There was just one more day with the crazy Kaminskis to go before Leonora Marino's bridal shower extravaganza was over, which meant make way for the groom.

My mother was clearly grateful Aunt Ginny had decided against some of the ideas her sister-in-law had pinned on Pinterest. Before the meal, my mother had taken me aside to show me Aunt Ginny's Instagram. "See this?" she zoomed into the snapshot on her phone. What I saw was too horrifying to fully set down in words, but it consisted of the shell of a watermelon filled with the disemboweled pulp of a cantaloupe. The cantaloupe had, in turn, been adorned with grapes for eyes and a triangle of kiwi for a mouth. Enveloping the top of the cantaloupe head were balls of honeydew and watermelon. The melon balls were, I supposed, intended to be curls. They were too spherical not to have been made with the precision of an ice cream scoop.

Never before had I known anyone so invested in turning food into something it was clearly not. Under the snapshot, ginny_007 had written:

#hermione'sbabyshower #bunintheoven
#toocutebabymelon #sorrymenopause

At supper, Vivian sat across from me, palms tee-peed in front of her. Her mouth was squirming, causing the veins marking the sides of her neck to dip slightly. Apparently, Vivian was just as primed to say "Grace" as she was to spit a projectile into my face.

I suppose she didn't know how to act around a cousin who increasingly thought of herself as an island adrift. Vivian, who studied my mother and me with a weariness that was equal parts captivation and disgust.

Despite the fervency of Vivian's stink eye, it was the first time in a while I'd been able to stay in the present, and keep the bad memories at bay. Though I actually listened to Uncle Tuck crack jokes while divvying the roast, I could not help but mull over how primitive it felt to celebrate my mother's forthcoming union over the consumption of that poor duck.

When it was time to unveil the Peep cake, Aunt Ginny began warding Uncle Tuck off. He—in an emphatic gesture that had occasioned Mythic Ethel to knock her glass over ("Lord love a duck," she tsked as she patted the table with a tissue)—came dashing back from the kitchen with matches and a fistful of candles.

"Dad, don't!" Vivian came alive again, her passion surmounting her stink eye, joining her mother in waving her hands urgently at Uncle Tuck, as if mother and daughter were divine seers warning against the advance of a very dark outcome.

"It's bad luck!" Aunt Ginny protested.

"Like toasting with water!" Vivian chimed.

Or wearing hot-ass ponchos to a bridal shower! I thought.

"We're celebrating your sister's future nuptials, not her birthday—get those candles away!"

"Ahoy!" Mythic Ethel clanked her teacup with her spoon, causing Charlize to make her palms into earmuffs.

Who would've thought superstition would be all the rage in the Kaminski house? The concern seemed more like one Leonora Marino would randomly spout, but my mother was getting into Uncle Tuck's plot, applauding as she told everyone else to shut up.

"Woo! Let's do it!"

So, despite half the party's protestations, Uncle Tuck covered Aunt Ginny's cake with candles.

"Would you look at that, Caboodle?" My mother drew her dog into her lap to see. "Isn't this something, Eva?" she gazed happily over the sea of burning candles, Caboodle looking Satanic as he gawped at me through the dancing light.

The awful part happened after the Peeps started to shrivel in on themselves resembling molten cheese, and all of a sudden, the entire cake caught fire, or so it seemed. Really, my mother's belled sleeve caught fire followed, somehow, by one of the tissue paper crowns the bride-to-be had left at each table setting.

While Aunt Ginny began smashing my mother's breasts with a chair pillow (I can't speak for how she thought this was going to serve any of us) I found myself stupendously aware that somewhere in the kerfuffle of dinner and candles, she and Uncle Tuck had taken off their ponchos. Perverse as it was in the moment, I wondered what their brilliant shades of neoprene lined with faux shearling would have looked like in the flames.

Regardless of the causes behind the fire, once started, it spread quickly. Before we knew it, the smoke alarms were going off and Mythic Ethel was expelling what sounded like a funeral hymn. Meanwhile, the mouth I remembered from childhood returned with a vengeance as Vivian tried to talk some "fucking sense" into us "fucking morons" by suggesting we "get the fuck out of this fucking mansion, there's a fucking fire, you fucking nitwits!"

She had obviously paid attention to the mandatory safety training we'd gone through in school, for before there was even time for the flames to reach their clothes, Vivian pulled her daughter into her arms and stopped, dropped, and rolled her way out.

Aunt Ginny was shepherding Mythic Ethel to safety, Mythic Ethel coughing up a storm and moving miraculously nimbly for not having her walker. But Uncle Tuck—*yoo-hoo, Uncle Tuck?*—where was he?

"C'mon, Eva!" Aunt Ginny shouted after me.

Call us crazy, but whether my mother and I were trying to reverse the disaster that had already ensued, or whether we had been waiting for the opportunity to do something momentous, when we were faced with the age-old challenge of fight or flight, we chose fight.

Our fight-response? We poured party cups of punch on the flames that swiftly climbed the curtains—half laughing, half sobbing at the mess that was our lives. The smoke was wafting up to the ceiling and all I could think was, *Smoke signals. Right!*

I was double-fisting party cups, deranged from the smoldering heat, telling myself to be not afraid, *You're the star in your own movie!* And besides, *this isn't just any old bungalow, this the widower Marino's beachfront bungalow, the one whose husband once owned Ship Bottom's favorite motels. Therefore, the bungalow can't burn down!*

Next thing I knew, I couldn't find my mother—"Mom?"—and then there was an awful crackling noise as some beam crumpled in the corner, and for a moment, I thought I heard someone shout, "Timber!"

I'd hardly noticed the sound of the alarm—there was so much flame trailing the curtains, so much smoke. The fire was like liquid, its blaze pouring over everything in the house—

Next, I heard the sirens blaring. Standing at the heart of the blaze while hacking up smoke, what I thought to myself was, *Don't worry, Eva, this can't be your life!*

A large boom soon followed as more wood splintered down, and I grabbed hold of my mother's hand, which felt oddly large and smooth—almost like a pelt or a glove. Was the fire ruining my sense of touch?

I looked over but couldn't see who belonged to the hand I was holding. Where was my mother? Where was Uncle Tuck? Windows shattered, glass crashed. There was a hail of white flakes. The hand I'd grabbed was pulling me along, but I didn't want to go, I couldn't find my mother—where was she?

I recalled the cover of the children's book *Are You My Mother?* with a just-hatched bird perched on a hound dog's forehead. *Are you my mother, oh hand that is pulling me along? I thought we were saving the bungalow, but maybe now it's going down into smithereens? Wasn't that a lovely cake Aunt Ginny baked for you, Mom? Are you having a nice bridal party?*

More smoke, my arm was bleeding—*what*—no! And then in between two of the dining room chairs I watched fold in on themselves from the flame, I thought I saw a woman's hands, reaching.

MOM? Through the smoke, I called out to my mother—I shouted and shouted, all the while trying to weasel from the hand that was pulling me out.

Uncle Tuck—there he was!—was trying to take hold of one of the firemen's hoses—or, wait, did I mean, "horses?" Uncle Tuck was trying to steal one of our rescuers' horses—

I couldn't make out more than a foot ahead, could no longer see the quilts patched from my old grade school clothes festooning the walls. Was that the hem of the jumper I wore when Sebastian first rolled on top of me, gently sliding my wrists to my sides as he smiled down at me?

Passing through tunnels of smoke, I wondered if there was a new door. Had a makeshift window to safety been axed? Who would've thunk a Peep cake could be the source of so much ash? Who in their right mind says the word, "thunk?"

"Eva! *Watch out!*"

Whoa, there, falling beam—you can't hit me! Now who was that coughing? Oh, hello. Hello, hand dragging me to nowhere.

Uncle Tuck, is that *your* hand that I'm holding? You started this mess—you'd douse things out, yes. *Right!* Because you, Uncle Tuck, have always had everything under control.

And good thing, too. Because all of a sudden, it felt like I was being dragged across continents and, at the same time, as if I were standing in place. Everything was spinning.

~~~

I was a little girl, Justina watching me over her cigarette, pans of hot apple dumplings bubbling.

I was standing on the edge of the rocks, holding Sebastian's hand, counting down from ten.

I was a freshman in college and my date was standing with me at my door, leaning in for a kiss while I closed my eyes and pretended that he was Sebastian.

I was barfing my brains out in a bathroom etched with profanities and vulgar doodles of SpongeBob. I was in the middle of texting Sebastian with my face over the toilet, while Arabella Busby held my hair back.

I was sitting on the edge of Finn's couch, an officer seated across from me. I was looking beyond him and out the window. The gulls flitting past as if everything were normal.

For a moment, far past the smoke and the fire, I thought I saw gates, then realized I was not going to heaven, not yet anyway, and the gates that materialized before me were not pearly, and there was no Dad or Sebastian floating atop angelic clouds, waving.

Dizzyingly, I soon came to realize that I'd mistaken the roughness of thick gloves for tufts of hair, as the hand that had been towing me transformed into a pair of arms pulling me into a stronghold, into a chest that smelled of sulfur and burnt plastic.

I turned in the direction of the hand that traveled from my wrist to my arm. My eyes narrowing on the glove to the neck to the helmet haloed by smoke.

Well, wouldn't you know, kind sir? I stared at the strange man holding me. *You've got a helmet on. Official!*

And though the fireman's mouth was set in a line, I could have sworn I heard him say, in a ventriloquist kind of way, "What is this, a death wish? Are you trying to destroy yourself?"
~~~

Chapter Twenty-two

You can imagine my surprise when I ran into Finn at our local grocery last winter and learned that he and Sebastian were renting a condo in Ship Bottom.

"Sebastian didn't tell you?" Finn ran his hand through his beard, surprised by his son's lack of communication. Or pretending to be surprised that, no, I hadn't known they were in town.

I ran my fingers through my hair like I normally did when I was uncomfortable. Before they'd moved away, Finn had earned his keep as a jack of all trades. Cutting trees and fixing sinks. Being fed and looked after, surely, by my mother's generosity. Father like son, Sebastian could never hold a job, he had always been a drifter. Last time we'd exchanged updates, Sebastian was in California, landscaping for wealthy people. I could only imagine what his and his father's livelihoods had become. The summer they moved out of Ship Bottom felt like eons ago. What were they doing here now?

"Something the matter, Eva?" Finn picked up a tomato and returned it to the pile. We were standing in the middle of the wide-open produce aisle and I suddenly felt very cold. A cold that didn't have to do with the frosty degree Marvin and Gully kept at their grocery.

"Nothing," I lied, forcing my hand down to my side. My confusion at having been left for years at a time in the dark eclipsed the prospect of seeing Sebastian. Though we were in the age of smartphones and social media—easy means of communication that neither Finn nor Sebastian were interested in—Finn and Sebastian still could have phoned or written. They had our landline and address. Good riddance.

Good riddance? I bit my lip. My thoughts were moving too fast. I was getting far too caught up in my anger. How could Finn so casually greet me at our local grocery, given the islands of silence between us? I mean, I was surprised he even recognized me!

I changed the subject. And it is with remorse, looking back on the fact, that I so offhandedly asked him, "Do you know about my father?"

Finn nodded gravely as he told me he had heard about "the tragedy" and had come to check on my mother.

But from whom had he heard it? From *Marvin and Gully?* I thought ruefully. It wasn't like Finn got *The Ship Bottom Chronicle* shipped to California. As far as I knew, Leonora Marino and he hadn't been talking. Or had they? Had my mother been keeping up with Finn even after he'd moved away? Of course not. It was impossible. My mother hadn't been the same in the years since Finn had left precisely because of the void his leave-taking made.

Where were you all that time? I wanted to shout at him. And, *It's a bit late for that. It's been four years since Dad passed. Where were you at the funeral? Where were you and Sebastian when we needed you?*

"Eva?" Finn swayed awkwardly from one heel to the other, looking as though he'd considered setting a hand on my shoulder, but then thought better. Returning instead to review the tomatoes.

"You rented a condo just to check on my mother?" I blurted. "That's why you're here?"

To which Finn replied, "Sorry, Eva. You know, I've just realized, I've got to go. See you around? We'll phone you. Sebastian will phone you soon. I'll tell him to." And, at that, he was gone.

It was shortly before the accident that Sebastian and I reunited—Sebastian did phone later, just like Finn said when I bumped into him.

During the years of distance, we eventually corresponded sporadically through email—my updates at first long and thorough, until to match Sebastian's responses, I altered mine to be short and straightforward. It took years of my sending him letters before this had happened. In our early twenties, we exchanged Christmas cards of hilariously satanic-looking Santas, and Valentine's Day hearts featuring hyperbolically beefy cherubs that seemed too encumbered by rolls to properly aim arrows.

Always, the exchanges between Sebastian and me were light and jokey. Like we were skirting around our having ever been together in all ways as children.

There are two things to know about the condo Finn and Sebastian were renting. The first is that it was where I am sure Finn made love to my mother before abandoning her for good. The second is that it ran on gas, which is important to keep in mind because it has everything to do with how, after Sebastian invited me over, texting from an unknown number—"Surprise! I'm here!"—I ended up in the condition that, given time and retrospect, I believe inspired Sebastian to ask me to follow him onto the rocks. It was after that night I ended up in the hospital that Sebastian changed. And by that, I mean he warmed to me. Something in him clicked, and he looked at me like he used to.

When I phoned my mother immediately after the uncomfortable exchange I'd had with Finn at the grocery, she was strangely quiet. It was hard to tell, over the phone, whether she'd known that Finn and Sebastian were back in town, or whether she was as put off by their arrival as I was.

After an initial beat of silence on the other end of the line, "When are you going to see him?" was, I believe, my mother's reply.

I left my apartment early to make sure the condo was where I thought that it was. Then, to pass the unnecessary extra fifteen minutes I had before our agreed-upon time—I couldn't just go knocking at their door—I drove a loop around the complex.

The condos were relatively new, and seemed out of place in the Ship Bottom I knew. I explored for a while longer before I found myself standing, bottle of wine in hand, on Finn and Sebastian's porch.

Though I was bundled up in my long black felt coat with the faux fur collar that my mother said gave me the air of Elizabeth Taylor, I was shivering. Whether this was because of the proximity of the coast amid one of Ship Bottom's blustery winters, or because I was anxious to see Sebastian, I can't be sure. But what I can say was that I was all nerves at the thought that at any moment Sebastian—the Sebastian I no longer knew—would swing open the door.

I had forgotten what a good cook Finn was. And the evening Sebastian invited me over to his and his father's condo for dinner—not extending, I noted, the invitation to my mother—the brown sugar baked salmon had been as delicious as the one I remembered from childhood. My nerves having dissipated somewhat after Sebastian and Finn greeted me at the door—Sebastian immediately cracking into the bottle I'd brought, and procuring us all full glasses—I was surprisingly able to relax enough to taste the food.

And the meal had started off almost like old times—even the flimsy card table Finn had topped with a tablecloth and drippy candles was the same as the one he'd had all those years ago, back at his beige cottage. The biggest difference was that my mother wasn't there, which meant the conversation was softer and more equally distributed among us. It also meant there was a lot less laughter. And while I puzzled over the fuzzy glow occasioned by the wine and the candles, I found I was grateful to be in Sebastian's and Finn's presence. And then shamed for feeling so.

My mother was the one who hadn't wavered; she was the one who had stood by my side.

And it was during these very conflicting feelings that, under the table, I felt Sebastian's knee graze mine and stay there. He or Finn must have made a tame joke afterward—I can remember laughing, lightly, wine glass in hand, feeling happy—when the beeping started.

Finn discovered that it was the carbon monoxide alarm that had gone off. "Fuck. There must be a leak in the stove."

And we all scurried around flinging open the door and the windows to get the fumes out.

After the alarm shut off and we'd aired out the apartment, Finn reheated our salmon loaf and cobbler, and the three of us assumed our places at the table laughing off the interruption.

"I'll bet there's a poltergeist in our midst. What do you say, Eva?" Finn winked across the table.

Watching *The Dark Knight* with Sebastian after supper, I kept thinking about Heath Ledger having recently been found dead in real life while, on screen, he marched around shooting everyone as The Joker. I was leaning against Sebastian's headboard, my plum-colored skirt spread over my lap, sitting close enough to Sebastian that our arms were just touching. We must have gotten twenty minutes into the movie before Sebastian reached up my skirt and I lost myself. It was when he started to kiss me that I began to feel sick—not because of the shock of what it meant to feel Sebastian again—but because something was wrong. I felt as if all the fish in my stomach was going to come up. My insides were turning. It was like I'd pulled my intestines from my mouth, and splayed them on the floor. Tiny dots filled my vision as I pictured a magician extracting a colorful stream of scarfs from his throat—

I must've blacked out, because suddenly, Sebastian was bringing me down the stairs and out the front door, carrying me over his shoulder. Had I been myself when Sebastian's valiant exertion occurred, I might have joked that I felt like a sack of yams or a slaughtered calf or what have you, but I was not myself. I was sick, and I was about to spill my guts in the snow.

Finn behind the wheel and Sebastian beside me, Finn whisked us to the ER because he and Sebastian thought I had carbon monoxide poisoning. From what I knew about carbon monoxide poisoning, I was either going to keep passing out from the toxins I'd absorbed, or puking until I really had impeded any chance of Sebastian ever wanting to be together.

It was later—after revolving glass doors, a beat in the Tiffany blue waiting room, and a visit with a bearded doctor—that I woke lying on a tissue paper-covered cot, wearing a smock the color of tater tots. And it is at this point that I can remember through the haze of that room that Sebastian was there. Leaning in close to whisper, *I love you, Eva.*

It was the first time he'd told me.

Chapter Twenty-three

"Sleeping like an angel," whispered someone who sounded like Aunt Ginny. Only poncho-clad Ginny Kaminski would speak a cliché like she'd come up with it herself.

I tried to move my neck from side to side, to get a grip on my body. Then there was a hand rubbing my arm that I wished would stop. I wrinkled my nose. Wherever I was smelled like air conditioning and cloves. I opened my eyes to my old Maine Coon Buttermilk blinking at me.

"What the—"

"She's awake!" someone shouted.

Who's awake? I wondered.

Buttermilk was pressing her furry face into my cheek, kneading my chest and purring before she was abruptly yanked off.

"Ow!" I cried as Buttermilk's claws dug into my skin.

"I told you this wasn't a good idea."

"Uncle Tuck?" I squinted at the hand rubbing my arm and traced it to the woman standing above me.

The woman's coiled red hair was dried into a kind of mat, like a slab of baked ziti long-forgotten in the oven. She was also wearing scrubs printed with pictures of Betty Boop posing in suggestive positions. Who the heck thought it was okay to go around with her hair looking like that? Not to mention, dressed like that? What startled me even more was the fact that I had mistaken her general presence for my long, lost cat. Nothing made sense.

"There, there," she coddled. "I'll let Doctor Raptis know you're up."

"Excuse me—*what?*" I tried to shift my head but there were too many pillows, it was like pillows were slowly devouring my skull.

"You'll let Doctor *What* know I'm up?"

"Ha-ha-ha!" Uncle Tuck laughed from the corner. "I made the same error! Doctor Raptis, not *Rapist*, Eva. You really should hold off before dropping that bomb on a victim of a recent trauma," he chided Betty Boop.

Betty Boop must have been in charge of wardrobe in whatever circle of hell I had woken. I was wearing a smock with sailboats. It was at that moment that the possibility that my lower extremities had been removed occurred to me. I wiggled my fingers and toes. *Thank God.* As a whole, I did feel rather jellylike in the way that many of Aunt Ginny's no-bake desserts tended to be—depending, as they did, on ruining perfectly good fresh fruit by drowning it in Jell-O.

"Hey there, Smokey," Uncle Tuck said, his face appearing where Buttermilk's had been. He was so close I could smell the vending machine coffee on his breath.

"Where's Mom?" I asked.

"I'm over here!" Leonora Marino called from somewhere beyond the fortress of pillows.

"Where—?"

"She's doing fine, don't worry." I wished Uncle Tuck would spare me his breath. Hadn't I been through enough?

What had I been through?

Betty Boop swooped in to brush the bangs from my face. What was with all this touching?

They're bangs, you cannot brush them away, Betty.

"The doctors are making me stay put. I'm all corded up," came my mother's voice. The image of which called to mind some freaky S&M stunt.

"When do you think she'll be better, Cleopatra?"

Cleopatra—who? I really had ended up in some other realm.

"Oh, she'll be fine once she—"

"You're Cleopatra?" I shouted at Betty. But she was busy taking my blood pressure, which I imagine had probably soared off the dial. Cleopatra or no, she was Betty Boop in my book.

"I went looking but couldn't find you," my mother was saying. "And then some firefighter fought me. I mean, he wanted to get me out, but there was no way I was leaving without my girl."

"When hasn't Leonora been the talk of Ship Bottom?" Uncle Tuck laughed.

"He called me hysterical!" my mother protested.

"That was *after* you split his lip," said Aunt Ginny.

"You're stronger than you look, sissy."

"Yeah, yeah . . ."

The Kaminskis' voices were coming from a galaxy far, far away. A galaxy where stars were replaced with pillows, and the night sky by a woman with baked ziti for hair who wore a shirt with portraits of a provocative cartoon character. Now, all I needed was my Yoda tree topper, and the Force would be returned.

"Where's Buttermilk?"

"Who's Buttermilk, Eva?"

"Buttermilk is Eva's dead cat."

"No, not Buttermilk. Sorry, I meant Mythic Ethel. Mythical Aunt Ethel."

"Our aunt isn't a myth," Vivian said with concern. Since when was Vivian in the room? "Our great aunt is—"

"Mythic Ethel is prancing with the unicorns at the Hilton," my mother said.

"No, the centaurs, Leonora."

"Stop it, you two!" Aunt Ginny, laughing, cried at Uncle Tuck.

But my mother's and uncle's tomfoolery was put on pause as the door to the room swung open and another woman appeared.

"Glad you're awake, Eva." The doctor with the ineffably criminal name introduced herself.

I jumped at the weight of cloth on my chest.

"I brought you something." Charlize placed my hand over Music Baby's cloth back, which felt very warm. Probably from Charlize holding onto her so long.

"Charlize, say 'excuse me,' honey," said Vivian.

"Isn't she a dear!" Doctor Raptis cooed.

"Cabbage says she wants you to get better quick, Eva," Charlize whispered.

Chapter Twenty-four

We were released from the hospital the next day and returned to yoga the day after that. Leonora Marino's bridal party having gone up in flames and a hospital stay be damned, my mother was adamant we not miss a class. Following our first class back, she was posting our whereabouts on her phone like always. Her latest hashtag was: #ThisMother&DaughterAreONFIRE. Which didn't seem to have the same ring as the Alicia Keys song, but I wasn't about to tell Leonora Marino that. I considered helping her carry something, but it wouldn't have been difficult if she weren't also on the phone. She looked burdened, hauling every yoga accessory you could think of. Amid the salty dim of another Ship Bottom summer, my mother could've been scaling the Appalachian Trail, purveyor of foam and elastic, terrycloth and cork, like some hunch-backed Scandinavian dwarf.

"Mom?" I nudged her, deciding that perhaps she'd realize how cumbersome the whole texting and walking tactic was, at which point I'd offer to help.

"Sorry, honeybun. I'm just sharing what Chastity was telling us about our breath."

My mother finished her tweet. "Hey," she said, "do you think Chastity's parents knew that their daughter was destined to become a yoga instructor when they named her 'Chastity'?"

"What makes you think 'Chastity' has anything to do with yoga?"

"Well," My mother thought about it for a moment, negotiating the strap of the yoga mat on her shoulder. "If 'pose of the child' is the route to Savasana, who better to act as your guide than a woman who goes by that name?"

"Maybe you're right. I mean, you named me after 'the fallen woman,' didn't you?"

"You're '*Eva,*' not 'Eve,'" She said as her phone chirped along to her post's comments and likes. "And I didn't name you after her."

"That's right. You named me after a Care Bear."

"No, after Eva Almos. For goodness *sakes,* Eva. Are you trying to make a wet blanket of your namesake? Eva Almos did the voice for Friend Bear, who isn't just any Care Bear, mind you. Friend Bear is the best of the cubs."

"Your Eva also did the voice of the bunny, right?"

"Don't be silly. *You're* my Eva!" My mother chided. Going on to remind me that it was Swift Heart Rabbit that I meant, and that Swift Heart Rabbit was among her favorites. After Friend Bear, that is.

Now that she'd officially put her phone away and was making a kind of elaborate hand gesture, it was obvious my mother wasn't ready to step away from the podium just yet. She was rearing up to elaborate. All I needed to do was humor her. Show some semblance of interest and the stage was hers.

"Why do you like Quick Start Rabbit?" I prompted.

"Well," my mother sighed dreamily, giving the question some serious thought. "She isn't a breakfast booster, honey. *Swift Heart* Rabbit lives in The Forest of Feelings, for one. Imagine that."

"I can't."

"Plus, she not only has that great heart and wing tattoo on her belly, but her fur is blue. Like, literally blue. Which seems like an oxymoron to me. Since she's supposed to be happy and loving, you know? The writers really got kids to think. They were smart, wouldn't you say?"

"I do say," I nodded. Proud that my mother was ignoring the vibrations from her purse. Maybe all it took was the Care Bears to get her to focus. At the end of Honeypot Road, whose name is perhaps the least thematically relevant in all of Ship Bottom, we moseyed on into our usual booth at The Grumpy Monk.

The local Sinatra impersonator performed every other Thursday, which was always a treat, and tonight was one of the every-other Thursdays our local Frank took the stage. My mother and I suspected that The Grumpy Monk arranged to have the act perform on Thursdays because the tavern wasn't as crowded. It was only the confused out-of-towners and die-hard patrons like me and my mother who came in on Thursdays, and apparently Frank wasn't the best at drawing customers. My mother and I decided it was a hearty blend of nostalgia and respect for Ship Bottom talent that kept the tavern's owners asking Frank to serenade their customers. When we arrived, he was doing a kind of finger-snap and hip-bump jig as he belted "Chicago!"

It was all very dizzying, what with the wall of enormous screens behind Ship Bottom's Sinatra, each tuned to a different soap opera or athletic competition broadcast in Spanish. By some twist of fate, The Grumpy Monk also got the Oxygen Channel, which meant reruns of *Oprah*. Goody! But the largest screen in the whole tavern filled the wall behind the bar, and that night, it was broadcasting a women's rugby game. One of the teams was wearing nude-colored shorts. It was unspeakably awful.

"We'll go for our usual," my mother told our waiter Jed.

Jed was half her age but that was okay. My mother enjoyed flirting with Jed, and Jed enjoyed flirting back. Plus, Leonora Marino was famed for leaving extravagant tips.

She was staring eagerly down at her sticky menu, which we mutually adored for its laminated photos of the meals. My favorite was the one of the fries smothered in "pub cheese." Which meant fluorescent Velveeta drenching the fingerlings like a highlighter pen had leaked all over them. In a certain light, the fries were so magnified, they looked porous.

My mother pointed to a photo that had the potential to give you nightmares. "Thoughts on 'Nacho Supremo'?"

"Nacho Supremo" seemed to possess the facial features necessary to make up a person, only they were made out of perishables.

"What about ice cream?" I pushed my menu aside and seized the list of dessert specials from behind the ketchup. The crust on the Heinz cap was disgusting, but it was just another reason I loved The Grumpy Monk. So many surprises! Some things for which there were no words. I studied "The Grumpy Sundae." The photo was obviously a heap of mashed potatoes capped in a toupee of chocolate topping, plus every kind of bonbon you could think of.

"You get that," my mother said. "I'm saying to hell with 'Nacho Supremo,' which obviously means bloating. I'm going to go with the wings. Boo-yah, protein!"

"Because you're an angel?"

"No, because you are, Eva. You're my Care Bear!"

I couldn't take my eyes off the photo of The Grumpy Sundae. "How many people do you think notice these are mashed potatoes?"

Leonora Marino frowned at the picture. "How can you not notice that those are mashed potatoes?"

"Did I hear someone say, 'Care Bears?'" Jed beamed as he dropped off our drinks. Jed was one of those guys who attempts to keep up with my mother and me and fails miserably. It was endearing, how he tried to be funny—be a Marino gal when there was only room for Leonora and Eva. Less endearing was how my mother encouraged poor Jed. All for her private amusement and to the detriment Jed would never begin to laugh at. My mother turned me into a downright jackal at The Grumpy Monk Tavern. Or maybe it was the additions of the Ship Bottom Sinatra and mojitos. Regardless, something about being there made me feel more honest, and therefore meaner.

"Cheers!" My mother raised her glass to mine and we clinked. My mother toasting with such gusto, some of the precious nectar that was our favorite cocktail slushed over the lip. The bartender had been particularly generous with the mint. Our glasses looked like aquariums with a disparate ratio of greenery to fish. Specifically a ratio disparate enough that the greenery had eradicated the fish.

It may have seemed backwards to flush our bodies with toxins after we'd just de-toxified ourselves at yoga, but Shiloh had told me to find a routine I was comfortable with and to stick to it. I'd told her all about my anxieties over making decisions, getting off my ass and drinking mojitos with my mother when my brain told me to stay in bed with the blinds drawn, the covers pulled over my head. *Go on, be that pad of butter on the potato. Melt,* said my inner ego.

My mother eyed our mojitos, arcing a brow in suspicion.

"You don't think that's kale, do you?"

"I wouldn't know. I refuse to eat anything that looks like stunted trees. Or bonsai. Like little cabbages confused for broccoli. One of those hybrids nobody knows the name of."

"The kind that tastes neither here nor there, but just ends up confusing your mouth," my mother nodded in earnest.

On the screen tuned to the Oxygen channel, Oprah was giving away a shit ton of free stuff, and all the glossy-faced women in the audience were clapping. Some of them were crying, they were so dang grateful to receive their free sparkle Uggs, which were hideous, if you asked me. But who's to say I'm the arbiter of great fashion? I was currently wearing stretchy pants with racing stripes and a Paddington Bear tank top. So, for all intents and purposes, *Go, Oprah go!*

My mother was already in the middle of pulling down her top to show me where she wanted to get her Swift Heart Rabbit tattoo.

"See here, child of mine. It's going to go right here . . ."

"*Mom!*" I batted the sight away with my hands. The Grumpy Monk was fun, but it wasn't Mardi Gras!

"Sorry," my mother smiled. She finished her drink and winked at adorably rotund and formal Lorenzo, who of all the servers at The Grumpy Monk, seemed like he would be more comfortable serving the bistro at The Four Seasons. A venue where they pulled your chair out for you and fluttered your napkin in your lap. Lorenzo was my personal favorite waiter at the tavern precisely because of his elevated behavior. Though neither a snowy white button-down nor black bowtie was part of The Grumpy Monk's uniform, Lorenzo always wore this outfit. Putting Jed and the rest of the wait staff to shame in their dumpy t-shirts emblazoned with the tavern's emblem of a monk gazing into a wishing well. Neither my mother nor I—or even any of the staff (we'd asked)—could figure out the meaning behind the insignia, which also appeared on the rotting sign hanging above the front door. On crowded nights when merrymakers piled into The Grumpy Monk to celebrate the milestone of one of its party's members, Lorenzo reminded me somewhat of Charlie Chaplain distributing Bud Light to pasty-faced men and Mai Tais to belligerent gaggles of singletons. His flourish of handing beverages to his sloppy patrons was always done with aplomb.

Jed reappeared to replenish our drinks. We didn't even have to ask; Jed always knew when to return with fresh ones.

After we placed our orders, Lorenzo flushed as he bowed away.

Leonora Marino was already making a dent in her second mojito.

It was impressive and scary how fast she could drink. Sometimes when we were out, I'd notice other women her age squeezing the stems of their Cosmopolitans between tight fingers as they observed her from afar. I didn't care how often my mother called attention to herself. No matter how you cut it, I'd rather have a guzzler for a mother than a woman who sipped her pink cocktail like a hummingbird futzing at a feeder.

My mother was pulling the mint from her glass and chewing it with her mouth open. I thought of cows going out to pasture while our Frank became increasingly excited over "Fly Me to the Moon." For this number, he was doing this unsettling hip thrust every time he said the word, "moon." Had he conflated Sinatra with Elvis?

"So," my mother pulled me from my reverie. "I have something I wanted to ask you about."

This can't be good, I thought.

"Yeah?"

"Yep."

"No!" I capped my mouth with my hand and giggled. My mother leaned forward.

"What?"

"You're making me nervous."

"My presence makes you nervous?" My mother was waving down Jed for yet another mojito. Get on the ball, Jed! "Blah-blah-blah!" My mother fisted the table. "There. You still nervous, Eva?"

"Go on," I laughed. The mojito must have hit me, because I suddenly felt giddy and gay in the way that only The Grumpy Monk Tavern's mojitos could make me. "What is it?" I asked.

"Well, you remember the wedding."

Wedding? What wedding? "Obviously," I smiled wryly.

"Well, I thought," my mother trailed, looking—was it possible?—slightly nervous, as well. "Seeing as the wedding preparations are in the bag and you're my daughter as well as my Maid of Honor. I—well—" she air-cheered Jed as he handed her another mint-packed mojito. Maybe the bartender thought the mint would soak up the alcohol? Save my mother and me from each other?

"What is it, Mom?" Elbows on the table, I set my chin in my hands and waited. "Just tell me."

"You might want to at least try to keep up with me on the mojito, darling," my mother channeled her best Lady Grantham.

"Okay . . ."

"Well, given that our home nearly burned to the ground—"

"That's an exaggeration. It was just the—"

"I was thinking we might as well get away for the weekend and go to the spa."

I coughed on my mojito, half-inhaling a sprig of mint. Lorenzo dropped my mother's chicken wings at our table, bowed, and receded into the shadows.

"But the wedding."

"Joining me at the spa would be your present to me. The wedding isn't until Monday, remember? Monday weddings are so outside the ordinary, don't you think?"

Yes. And yours and Ted Turbine's marriage will be anything but ordinary, I nodded in agreement.

"What about Caboodle?" I asked.

My mother was already making a mess, dunking a wing into the Ranch, making puddles of dressing. What happened to my Grumpy Sundae?

"Uncle Tuck's already offered to take him."

"That's far for Caboodle to go. I mean, all the way to Lancaster? Caboodle gets carsick. He—"

"What—are you afraid Lancaster will corrupt him or something? Teach Caboodle to bake bread from scratch, steer the horse and buggy? Tuck and the rest will all be back for the wedding anyway, Eva. It's not a big deal."

"I thought you hated spas."

"Part of me does. They remind me of my childhood."

"I'm not even going to ask what you mean by that."

"Think towels and robes. Clean, white terrycloth. You know how everything had to be clean at your grandmother's all the time. It's like it didn't matter that we grew up by the ocean. Tracking sand in meant germs and death. I'd come in from a swim and your grandmother would accuse me of smelling like a fish. And she'd spout off specific kinds, too. Like she could distinguish the pong of a marlin from that of a guppy. So anyway, what do you say to a mother-daughter spa trip?"

I thought about all the money my mother had been spending after Dad passed. Honestly, she'd been spending like water. Or like a man with no arms. Wasn't that a fable?

It didn't help that my mother was also a sucker for infomercials. Like, any of the ones where the man selling the apple pie-scented toilet bowl cleaner is shouting in your face.

"Well?" Leonora Marino was getting anxious. Why so desperate for a spa trip? But then again, why not?

"Is it expensive?" I asked.

"Of course it is."

"Do we—you. I mean you. Do you have enough for this?" I was feeling the mojitos, and where was my sundae? It was last call at the bar, and Sinatra was on his final number, "Ain't that a Kick in the Head." I counted the empty glasses on the table. How long had we been here?

"I don't have any money, Mom," I said.

"Which is why I'm treating *you*. And why you're going to move back into the bungalow," she burped. "Now that *that's* settled, we can decide on our treatments. You'll sign up for a Paraffin Bath with me, won't you? Those paraffins. They're so cute, you know?"

"I think you're thinking of puffins."

My mother was glaring over my head.

"Goddamnit!" She wagged a tortilla chip at one of the screens. The one behind me was playing *The Bold and the Beautiful,* Leonora Marino's second favorite show, *Downtown Abbey* being her first. A blond woman was throwing a chair at a brunette. It was like Betty and Veronica gone crackers.

"Eric Forrester is having an affair again," my mother was saying. "Way to shit on the whole arc, Eric! Good riddance!"

When I turned back around, she was frowning. "Honey, where in the name of Ship Bottom is your ice cream?"

When Jed and Lorenzo eventually came around with my sundae, my mother and I were plastered.

"Wait a second," I spit my first spoonful back into my bowl. "This really is mashed potatoes!" I glared at Jed.

Lorenzo threw his hands over his face and fled for the kitchens.

"It's his specialty," Jed glanced over his shoulder to assure that Lorenzo was out of earshot. "He said he got it from some magazine called *Eat Right!* More like 'Eat Shit,' huh? I don't blame you, Miss Marino. I'll nab you a piece of The Monk's famous tiger cake and throw in a kahuna coffee, on the house. How's that sound?" At which point Jed, in another attempt to indoctrinate himself into my mother's and my club, curved his hands into claws, and yelled, "Rwar!"

Chapter Twenty-five

I was in the third grade, I think, when Sebastian borrowed the storybook called *The Drowned Mermaid* from the school library. It was the illustrations and the premise that had us paging through it over and over, so enthralled were we by this idea that a mermaid could drown.

What the whole plot boils down to is this: all the little mermaids who live in their glittery palaces under the sea are popular and fun-loving and own colorful turtles. Then one day, when the pink-finned mermaid's best friend doesn't notice that her BFF is drowning, and instead swishes off merry and composed with the other mermaids; when the pink-finned mermaid is trying to pull her blind, pet turtle from the weeds he is lost in, she feels a shadow loom above her. Quick as a wink, a mesh falls over the mermaid, and before you know it—caught in the net the fishermen eventually abandon—the pink-finned mermaid lies trapped at the bottom of the sea, singing to herself as the days go by.

Eventually, in an ending I still can't quite wrap my head around, the pink-finned mermaid dies of loneliness or maybe lack of food, it isn't clear. From her point-of-view, I imagined it must have been like clawing at a glistening web. As if she had become a butterfly bound within its silk chrysalis.

The story is sort of like that fable, "The One-Eyed Doe," when in the end it's all about the doe getting shot while trying to look in multiple directions, and as the moral tells us, trouble is smarter because it comes from the direction we least expect it.

~~~

Just before Sebastian and Finn moved away—not thinking, really, but going on sheer impulse—I took the book about the drowned mermaid from the library without checking it out. Then I tore the book in half, giving Sebastian the sad and romantic ending of the story and keeping the first and happier half for myself.

Obviously, I hadn't known at the time how the decision to take the book would affect my understanding of Sebastian's death. At the time, I thought I knew everything there was about what it meant to love someone.

But I was just a child, and the book-tearing and stealing happened before I knew heartache. Before I found the woman in the shimmering skirt writhing inside The Barrel of Monkeys the night my mother, the Kaminskis, and I went to the carnival. Before I preserved the part of the mermaid's story I wanted for myself, and gave away the tragic half of the stolen book.
~~~

Chapter Twenty-six

The Copperhead Spa and Resort was taking far longer to get to than I'd been prepared for. Not that anything involving Leonora Marino could ever be prepared for. We'd started the drive out that morning and the shadows were already gathering. Having gotten our fix at The Grumpy Monk, my mother refused to go back to the bungalow—insisting it would depress her and suggesting we instead spend a night at the Holiday Inn. Seeing as we realized we only had the yoga outfits Uncle Tuck brought us when we were discharged from the hospital, on the way to the spa, my mother suggested we make a detour to the outlets. There, my mother purchased for us gauzy cotton shirts, boat shoes, and bandanas from The Gap, and a selection of J. Crew Bermuda shorts in ice cream parlor shades.

"I wonder if the Copperhead offers some kind of snake skin treatment," my mother said. Tooling around on her phone with one hand and manning the wheel around the narrow turns with the other. Was she really trying to get cell service in the middle of the Catskills?

"Stop it, you're driving!" I swatted her phone.

My mother let the phone fall in my lap as she went on to describe a treatment of her invention that involved applying hot wax to the bottoms of the feet and using snakeskin to tear off the callouses.

"Or maybe The Copperhead *serves* snake. "What part of our organic, free-range water moccasin would you ladies like?" my mother mimed. "The fang or the rattle?"

We arrived at the spa looking like we'd just spent a total of five hours in Leonora Marino's convertible with the top down, the mountain air whipping our hair to and fro, because that's what we'd done. For all my mother's fantasies—from the outside, at least—The Copperhead Spa and Resort was not at all snake-festooned as I knew she hoped it would be.

"Where are the stone cobras?" she demanded, pulling into the cul-de-sac that was far too in line with Martha Stewart and Co. to mitigate the eccentricities of Leonora Marino.

It was while she was muttering something about hoping the spa at least offered a venom bath scrub that out of blazing nowhere, a trio of valets wearing black surrounded my mother's BMW like ninjas. One valet retrieved our bags and went zipping off with the convertible to park it, while the other two appeared to be my mother's and my personal escorts. One on either side, they walked us straight to the door, a hand at our forearms. I felt like I had been taken back into the time of Jane Austen, the English countryside replaced with aggressively groomed rock gardens.

Boy-men—that was my impression of The Copperhead's staff. It was like being surrounded by Eagle Scouts on testosterone pills. Eagle Scouts with arrestingly crotchy pants.

The Copperhead's foyer was chockful of chakra bowls and trickling fountains. It was, I realized, the kind of place in which I would not have been surprised to see a celebrity float by. Recovering between box office flops at a setting where you could strike a chakra bowl whenever you were moved to do so.

"Look at those, Eva," my mother nodded at the lineup of chakras. "Footbaths in the hallway!"

From there, in accordance with my mother's suggestion, the Eagle Scouts gave us a glimpse of the swimming pool and aerobics facility; the rows of "wellness nooks" and the taxidermy-filled library, whose selection of books was overwhelmed by the walls of antlers and pelts. There was even a stuffed jackrabbit head that looked suspiciously like Benjamin Bunny, his tam ditched in favor of horns.

Thankfully, the receptionist wasn't required to dress like the valets. Instead, to behold the receptionist was like coming across a dog-owner who is the spitting image of her labradoodle, except in this case, there was no labradoodle in sight to compare her to. Regardless, I had the feeling that somewhere in The Copperhead Spa and Resort lurked a labradoodle that belonged to this woman.

"I'm Dot!" The receptionist smiled with her whole mouth.

I'm Period! I was tempted to shout back. Better yet: *I'm Colon!*

My mother checked us in with the warm, bubbly flair that was classic of her in the presence of strangers.

After Dot led us to the elevator, she gave us room keys and tote bags filled with Copperhead-related swag. There was a water bottle that said, "Awaken Your Mind: You've Arrived!"; an activity schedule for which a binder was necessary to keep all the pages together; a stress ball and a sweatband; an apple stamped with a "Have a Mindful Day!" sticker.

"It's a scratch-and-sniff," Dot giggled at the sticker. "Smells like Kombucha!"

Less than hour into our stay, as we commenced our detoxification at the fizzy water bar, my mother and I agreed that everybody at the Copperhead Spa and Resort appeared to be recovering from something.

The furniture at each pristinely laid table in the spa's dining room consisted of thrones, the arms and backs chiseled with mahogany serpents wreathed about apples. At dinner, whenever I sat back, a tree limb or snakehead stabbed my shoulder. Finally, an allusion to snakes!

I smeared my dinner roll with butter. "I feel like this chair was meant for me."

"Wait!" my mother held up her hand. "Hold that thought—the back of my throat is clogged with goat cheese," she coughed. "That's better. Now, what?"

Just at that moment, one of the half dozen waiters in charge of our table sprung from the brickwork and began de-crumbing our places.

"You were saying?" My mother prompted after they'd gone.

"I was saying that I'm sitting at a chair carved with serpents and fruit. I was saying that I'm Eva, which means this chair was meant for me."

"Oh, not this again. For the last time, I didn't name you for The Risen Woman."

"You mean 'fallen.'"

"No, no, no. Adam fell down and Eve came tumbling after. Everyone just looks for reasons to blame women, but in fact, we keep the ball rolling—if you know what I'm saying. Hence, 'The Risen Woman.' We rise like yeast." My mother dabbed her mouth. "Sylvia Plath. She said something like that."

The waiter came by with our lobster stuffed with crab stuffed with haddock. When my mother thanked him for the "seafood ménage à trois," he didn't laugh like Jed would have. My mother's audience was much more reliable at The Grumpy Monk Tavern.

"Guess he never learned French!" my mother said while the waiter was still standing there.

By the time we were on our fourth and final course, my mother had me in stitches. Dessert at The Copperhead Spa and Resort apparently meant mousse the color of Buttermilk's vomit. Which is to say, the color of buttermilk.

"Look. A volcano," I prodded the mound and it jiggled. "Oh, it's flan!"

"So lifelike!" my mother whacked hers with deliberateness.

Before she'd even swallowed her first bite, my mother decided the flan tasted like socks. "Band camp socks!" she pounded the table. "That's exactly what it tastes like! The kind tuba players march the quad in!"

"Mom!" I was seriously concerned the flan was going to come up my nose. I couldn't stop laughing.

"Eva," she leaned forward. "Have you ever seen those medieval depictions of the serpent with a woman's face for a head?"

"Nope," I said. Trying to reign in my laughter. Apparently, we weren't yet over the subject of Eve.

"The serpents with the female heads. You should see them, Eva.

"Sounds like something from *Goosebumps.*"

My mother's eyes lit up. "Our lives are like something from *Goosebumps*—your dad's cardiac arrest and your best friend's drowning all in a span of five years. To think how much we've lost—it scares me, you know? And now I'm marrying a man who runs a jumble sale of Nissans every day of the year." My mother paused to push away her flan.

Planting her forearms on the table, she said, "You okay, honey? Gosh, I wish you could see yourself. What are you thinking? You're thinking about something terrible, aren't you? Yes, Eva, you look like you're about to fall off the face of the Earth. Was it something I said?"

Chapter Twenty-seven

Our first full day began with quinoa pancakes topped with clover honey and butter made from dairy alternatives. Afterward, my mother signed us up for virtually every event possible.

Hitting the chakra bowls in the foyer afterward for kicks, a poster advertising a "Spirit Animal Dream Workshop" caught her eye. The poster showed Dilly, the teacher, looking way too comfortable and Zen-like in a headstand that gave me a headache just to look at. On either side of this accomplished spirit animal dreamer were rows of gargantuan timpani drums.

My mother held up a hand. "Don't even think of saying no!" she said.

A woman with a striking widow's peak and the smoothest complexion I'd ever seen was the only one other than my mother and me to show up for Dilly's workshop.

Carla offered her name with the most pronounced New Jersey accent I had heard since my stint interviewing contestants for Ship Bottom's annual corndog-eating contest as part of my internship at *The Ship Bottom Herald*. It was hard not to gape at Carla, on account of her smooth skin and her widow's peak, which could have given the likes of Mickey and Minnie a run for their money. The fact that her tar-black hair was slicked back into what looked like a painfully tight ponytail did not temper the effect. Was the shine of her raven's mane a normal feature? Or was Carla the victim of chronic oily-scalp syndrome?

"Have you gals done this before?" Carla asked us excitedly. My mother was occupied searching for Dilly. Peeking over the racks of stretchy bands and bocce balls as if she expected Dilly to be waiting in hiding, ready to pounce on her brave volunteers.

"Never!" I said. "Have you?"

"Tits, no!" Carla beamed.

I was still recovering from the collision of Carla's shiny face with her word choice when Dilly floated into the room, bringing with her the smell of lemongrass and beeswax. My stomach growled, and I realized the odor particular to Dilly occasioned my sudden craving for Thai food.

"Hello," she said, raising her hands palm-side up, as if she were balancing an invisible platter. She wore a necklace with a rock so substantial, I half expected her to crumple from the weight of it. But then again, the existence of a teacher in spirit animal dreaming defied all expectation.

"My name is Dilly, and today I'm going to guide you into the spirit realm, where—if you're patient and fortunate enough—your spirit animal will expose itself."

"Expose?" my mother hissed to me from the side of her mouth. "As in, flash us? Turn us into—"

"Carla," Dilly whispered with half-closed eyes.

"Yeah?" Carla said blankly, brow raised.

"Leonora," Dilly inhaled deeply as she drew her hands over her head, pressing the palms together into a tepee.

"Eva," she exhaled, drawing her hands back down. I thought of Chastity, back at Fountain-of-You Yoga and what I'd have paid to see her and Dilly try to breathe in the same room. There'd be no more air left for anyone else.

When Dilly opened her eyes, I pictured her as a snowflake softly kissing the concrete. She began distributing eye masks and Alpaca foot-booties, blankets printed in designs from olden tribes. When it was all said and done, and Carla, my mother, and I were lying on our mats—masked, booteed, and blanketed—I imagine we looked about as content and frightened as those travel ads you see of vacationers absorbing an exotic place's local flavor.

I wondered how many others had lain on these blankets in the hopes of accessing the tunnel through which, according to Dilly, we accessed our animal spirits.

Easing us into our realms, Dilly told us to imagine a color we could "fold ourselves into," a directive that occasioned me to fear this being some Freudian stunt—one by which we were encouraged to access our mother's womb and what not. A request that would be upsetting under any circumstance, but particularly so, given that, A) my mother was booteed and blanketed right beside me, and B) the idea of Leonora Marino having to in any way channel my grandmother would scare the living daylights out of my mother. She could easily be pushed into convulsions. That's just how fragile my mother's relationship with Grandma Kaminski was.

"Relaxxxx," breathed Dilly. "Picture your color. Folddd yourselves into that color."

I sighed and went along with Dilly's exercise. Imagining blue. Fields of cotton candy blue . . .

As soon as Dilly turned on the recording of the drums to help guide our spirit animal interview, I was snatched from the pleasant trance. All I could see through the layers of tissue and eye mask were a family of Claymation raccoons. Perched on ottomans in the ornamental style of ancient Eastern empires, I found them shoveling pancakes into their mouths when I reached them.

It was useful, being somewhere else. And the spa felt galaxies away. The only water near the property was chlorinated or else pumped into a manmade swamp. In short, it seemed like the perfect setting for us to recoup.

And like her bridal shower, my mother's plans for a mother-daughter getaway were going swell. Following our spiritual animal workshop—"You mean, 'exorcism'?" my mother answered Carla after Carla asked how my mother had liked the class—my mother and I spent the rest of the day kayaking, drinking smoothies, and being treated to hot stone massages by Lars and Napoleon, who contended that, yes: those were their real names, and of course the stones they were pushing into our trapeziuses had been blessed by the gods of the Delaware River. We were on holy grounds at The Copperhead Spa.

But then, after our massages and a spell in The Whisper Room, a sanctified space dedicated to meditation and personal reflection—"Help yourselves to the cucumber water and organic granola and trail mix, but please refrain from talking louder than a whisper"—my mother seemed different. Like her time of private reflection had soured her mood. For it was while we were walking down to the dock, trying to get feeling back into our muscles—Lars and Napoleon had really taken it out of us—that my mother stopped in her tracks. Frowning, she pointed to the tree arcing over the path, its trunk suspended like an upside-down letter "u."

I said it was a sign of good luck, the horseshoe-shaped trunk, but my mother stood by her original reaction, which was that the tree was sick, a reminder of drought and decay. In other words, what comes into the world will eventually become too thirsty to sustain itself. All it can do is hollow and rot.

Chapter Twenty-eight

Seeing as we kept bumping into the only other person ballsy enough to take the spirit animal dream class with us, we ended up not only becoming friendly with Carla, but learning the ins and outs of The Copperhead Spa from her.

My mother and I wanted to know more about the facial Carla said was the secret to her mirror-clear complexion. Leonora asked, "What did they do to your face to make it like that—cake it in oatmeal?"

"They extract all the goop from your pores."

"Goop?"

"Goop!" Carla's widow's peak bobbed right along with her head as she nodded. Not in the least distressed when my mother asked if she could please touch her forehead. If anything, Carla was honored.

"Touch ahead!" she offered her forehead to my mother's eager hand.

For our second afternoon, Leonora Marino scheduled a bird-watching class that Carla was also taking. Among the highlights of the class was that we got to wear binoculars and fanny packs. The latter carried only bird identification pamphlets and acai gummy worms, and were thus basically unnecessary.

To top it off was the fact that our guide Rupert had eyebrows so unruly—the long, curling follicles bushed out into directions I didn't know it was possible for hair to grow into—they mimicked a bird of prey's.

"I dost believe I spy a great horned owl!" my mother loud-whispered in her Lady Grantham voice to me and Carla, turning to the photo of the bushy-browed hoot owl in her pamphlet and comparing it to Rupert.

After bird-watching, Carla had to jet off for her fish pedicure.

"Do I even want to know?" I said.

"Sure you do!" said Leonora, who was thankfully in a better mood that afternoon than she'd been the evening before. "Do tell, Carla!"

"Well," Carla's shiny face flushed, reveling in my mother's attention, "the fish sort of suck off the dead skin from your feet, and—"

"Get the picture!" I interjected.

"No need to shout, darling," my mother laughed, wheeling on Carla. "Now Carla, I was thinking we'd have salmon for dinner. You'll join us, won't you? I want to see your feet after the fish-sucking is all said and done."

To round off the afternoon, my mother managed to squeeze us into a terrarium-making class taught by a teenager named Apple. Though she wore a frilly gingham apron, daisy earrings, and her frizzy long hair in braids—traits I associated with the quintessence of innocence—it was clear that Apple would rather eat a stick of butter than teach us fools how to make our own terrariums. When she introduced the materials we were using, distinguishing each type of soil and moss with fake cheer, she obviously struggled not to scowl at my mother, who kept interrupting to ask questions.

Other participants included a very tan couple, who resembled the actors in the Snuggies commercials. I'd thought this couple's constant touching and lovey eyes gave them away as honeymooners, but my mother was quick to point out that neither was wearing a ring: "Tryst Ken and Barbie," she said behind her hand.

The remaining pair in sour Apple's class included a recently divorced guy with a receding hairline and his mother, whose platinum-colored permanent and Cupid's bow mouth, drawn on with bright orange crayon, gave the impression of a 1950s pinup who refused to drop her look decades after she modeled.

The divorcee was openly drinking wine when he and his mother came in, and was clearly sozzled before the terrarium how-to began. When, at the end of her introduction, Apple had invited questions, he asked if broken hearts could be planted in terrarium soil: "I'm trying to get a jump-start on my ex's Christmas present!" By the time Apple tried to correct his ratio of sphagnum moss to pebble, he had already moved on to the hard stuff. "Bikini on the rocks," he said incomprehensibly to me, cramming even more moss into his terrarium pot when Apple wasn't looking. Before Apple even got to show us how to nest our succulents into the soil, his mother had to escort him out—"I'm gonna blow chunks!" he exclaimed, just before his hands flew to his mouth.

After the class, the corridor smelled of eucalyptus oil, laundry detergent, and vomit. My mother waited until Barbie and Ken went traipsing off before heading for the divorcee and his mother, who were seated on a large black couch printed with bamboo and tropical flowers. It wasn't clear who was comforting whom, but there was a good deal of back-rubbing and nose-blowing going on.

"Bob," the divorcee said when he noticed my mother standing over him. "Don't worry, I used soap," he added sheepishly, extending his hand.

"Hello, Bob." My mother shook his hand and turned to his mother. "I'm Leonora and this is my daughter Eva. That was a trip in there, wasn't it?" She indicated the room Apple was emerging from. Apron off and braids undone, a bag of moss slung over her shoulder, Apple looked like the spawn of Father Christmas.

"Leonora and Eva," Bob's mother repeated. Somehow, perhaps in the chaos that was her son's barfing emergency, she'd managed to smudge her lipstick.

"This is my mother, Minnie," Bob offered.

"Minnie and Bob," my mother repeated, winking at Minnie. "Well, Minnie and Bob. Eva and I wanted to ask if you'd join us for dinner. We've got one more in our party. Her name's Carla and she's a real doll. We'd love if you came along!"

~~~

Before our promised fish dinner with the others, my mother wanted to find the labyrinth she had seen on the map of The Copperhead's property.

I could tell a storm was coming—the evening was humid and boggy, odorous of honeysuckle and damp soil. You could cut the air with a spoon.

The labyrinth at The Copperhead consisted of a swirling pattern of red bricks amid a field of gray ones. Not what I had envisioned at all, which was more in line with a towering hedge. Apparently, you were supposed to follow the red brick path, which my mother and I did, until we found the center of the labyrinth. At which point, what was once lost, my mother affirmed, was now found.
~~~

Chapter Twenty-nine

We had all just received our Jail Island Salmon when my mother's cell phone went off, and MC Hammer's "U Can't Touch This" rallied off the dining room's walls.

"It's Tuck!" my mother informed us, worried and excited at once. "Hello?" she shouted into her phone, oblivious to the stares from the diners not sharing our table. "That's wonderful, Tuck. Just marvelous!" My mother dug into her salmon, flicking bits of tabbouleh as she continued to happily shout into her phone, and not only between mouthfuls.

From what I could grasp from her side of the conversation—"That's great the old bean is no longer angry with us, Tuck! It wasn't like the fire was our fault—who would've thought we'd have a writer in the family? Excluding my lovely daughter, that is!"—Uncle Tuck phoned to inform my mother that the events of my mother's bridal shower weekend had inspired Mythic Ethel to write the memoir she'd always wanted to write.

I looked around the table. At Carla, who was shoveling tiny, inordinately fast bites into her mouth as she watched my mother with a level of concentration I associated with viewing a particularly gripping episode of *The Bachelor*; at Bob, who'd set his fork and knife on the edge of his untouched plate as he regarded my mother with the kind of expression I had seen countless times on the faces of the men Leonora Marino enchanted.

I glanced away quickly. It embarrassed me to see my mother ogled—not that I blamed the array of men who did—my mother was so charming, so openly flawed and so human. She made it easy to love her.

"Har-har-har! Very funny, Tuck! Very funny! The Old Bean couldn't be telling the truth about that, now! She just couldn't!" My mother was squealing, wiping the wine dribbling down her chin with the back of her hand.

Bob's mother was sitting so still I started when I glanced her way. She was looking at my mother with something like recognition. I didn't even bother masking my stare; as far as Minnie was concerned, my mother and her son were the only ones in the room. And so, I watched Minnie's eyes ping-pong between Leonora and Bob. She was evaluating the situation, interpreting her son's interest, and, it seemed, disapproving.

As the lights in the dining room dimmed, the merry-making sounds of fiddles and pipes began to stream through the loudspeakers. The melody was one that belonged to the genre of music common in the land of the fairies.

I smelled the woman before I noticed her. The aroma was something like coconuts and grass skirts. She smiled and cleared her throat at the same time—treating us to a real talent. I hadn't known it was possible to utter such a pronounced noise while grinning, especially given that the woman's throat-clearing was more like a croak. Fittingly, she wore a flower in her hair and a flowy maxi dress whose print looked more suitable for an edition of *Leaves of Grass.*

I raised a brow at the flower in her wavy black tresses as she smiled harder and made the noise again.

Noticing our visitor, my mother cupped her hand over her phone's mouthpiece and batted her lashes. "Family emergency!" she mouthed to the woman. Her head bobbing along to whatever Uncle Tuck was saying.

The woman pressed her lips together, prepared to say something, but then stopped.

Even as the words left my mouth, I couldn't believe I had the nerve to think, not to mention utter, such a terrible farce: "My aunt just died," I told her.

It was amazing, the things I'd do for my mother. Even when she was in the wrong, something inspired me to protect her, and at the time, it seemed right to lie for her.

After the woman nodded solemnly, apologizing profusely before stumbling away, my mother pushed her plate away. Offering the table a wave as she prepared to carry on her conversation with Uncle Tuck in the hall. I shoveled in a couple forkfuls of salmon and followed suit. Rolling my eyes and shaking my head to indicate my exasperated *This is normal for my mother* expression.

As Carla squealed her goodbyes and I gathered my shawl, I lingered just long enough to see Minnie give her son's forearm a squeeze.

After my mother got off the phone with Uncle Tuck, she drifted out past the lobby and into the dark. "Coming, darling?" she called over her shoulder, though she wasn't waiting for me to catch up to her, either. So I trailed behind a bit, put on my shawl, and watched her take off. Her Pashmina billowing softly, sail-like, behind her, as she padded down to the water, the creaking cypress trees velvety all around her. She paused at the edge of the lake, crossing her arms and only half-looking at me. We hadn't ventured to this side of the water at The Copperhead before. We'd gone down to the docks to kayak, traipsed along to go birdwatching, but my mother had managed to lead us down a new path. And in the dark, no less.

"Care to lie down?" She nodded at the hammock strung between two cypress trees.

"You know," she said as we settled in with the ropey mesh swaying between us and I gazed up through the trees, "hammocks always look comfortable. I mean, when you see others in them. In the movies, they always seem like a dream. But really, I kind of feel like Tarzan. Or George of the Jungle. Don't you?

"Mom?" The hammock jostled as I turned. I gazed at my mother's finger where the engagement ring from Ted ought to be. Up until he asked my mother, she'd continued to wear the wedding band she'd had from Dad. Then, for a time, she'd worn both rings—the wedding band from her dead husband; the engagement ring from the man slated to become her new one. And now, at The Copperhead Spa and Resort, days before her wedding, her finger was bare.

"Are you feeling okay, Eva?" my mother answered my trembling voice. "It wasn't the fish, was it? I don't even remember eating mine, but—"

"Mom," I stared hard at her beautiful hands, her naked fingers.

I detected what smelled like burnt marshmallows. The fire pit crackling in the distance, the ghost of a woman's laugh.

"Were you ever in love with Dad?" I asked.

Chapter Thirty

A breeze rustled my bangs over my eyes and I batted them back. It was warm outside, but I felt chilled—my mother was taking too long to answer. Out of instinct, I felt my pocket for my phone, thinking of Shiloh. What would she say if she were watching my mother and me now? I wondered if word had got out about our bungalow's fire—I certainly hadn't told her, and imagined the coffee plant I'd bought at my last appointment would be drying up, dropping its leaves. I'd left it back at my apartment for days.

"Of course I did," my mother's voice sent me reeling back. "I loved your father. I always loved your father."

"But only him?"

"I loved your father," she repeated.

"Okay, I get that." I sighed, still eyeing my mother's hands. The fingers twisting together—what was she holding? A tissue? The end of her Pashmina? "But were there others?"

"You know me, Eva."

"Who?" I pressed.

"Well," my mother adjusted herself in the hammock. "There was Finn, to start," she said simply. Daring me to question her, to ask her more. The secret from my childhood that had never been a secret. The unspoken, finally spoken so plainly.

That my mother had tagged "to start" onto her admission struck me. I allowed the thought to settle as an onslaught of memories came like sand through a sieve. Not long before I ended up heaving half a salmon loaf out the window of his car on our drive to the ER, hadn't Finn said something about how good it was to have things back to normal?

What did Finn mean by "back to normal"? "Normal" as in back in Ship Bottom? Or "normal" as in life without my father?

"Mom?" I said suddenly, my voice lost in the dark, "How long did you know Finn?"

"He lived down the road from us since you were a kid."

"No, I mean . . . did you know him before Dad?"

"Of course," my mother said without a beat. Stating a fact that we had never talked about as if it were obvious. My mother's tone natural as telling the waitress, "Yes, I'll take fries with that, please."

"But he never asked you to marry him," I guessed.

My mother gazed mistily up into the trees. "No," she rolled onto her side. "No. But it doesn't matter. That didn't matter. There was always . . ."

"Always what, Mom? Always who?"

My mother curled herself into a ball. Her face to the ribbon of black water, her back to me.

"Sebastian," she whispered. "Sebastian . . ."

"What about Sebastian?"

I was prepared for her to tell me Finn was my father, making Sebastian and me brother and sister, or something equally fucked up. But then I thought back to that wedding photo with Dad my mother kept on the mantel, tallied the years, and realized that would have been impossible. The truer revelation being that when Dad and she had married, my mother must have already been pregnant with me.

"Sebastian," my mother whispered. "I loved him too, Eva."

My mother's words quaked the ground. Filling my ears was something like the sound of a thousand wings beating. I could feel the roots of the trees—or the ground, something—buckling. How often had it happened—once? Twice? Throughout my childhood?

Your mother is a good person, Sebastian once said. *She'd never try to hurt anyone.*

And now I understood what he meant.

"You're the worst person," I said, shaking the terrible images from my head—those replacing my memories of finding my mother entangled with Finn, with those of her with Sebastian instead. "You are the worst person," I said again, louder. "The very, very worst."

I swung my legs over the edge of the hammock so quickly I nearly dumped my mother out.

"Hey!" she cried.

I picked up the stone before I knew what I was doing and drew my arm back. I felt the cold edges of it, then heard the whoosh of it, and then I charged through the brush, dizzied and breathless. Leaves hissing in the trees and the sticks cracking underfoot, the cypress boughs scraped across my cheek as I swallowed the cry that rose in my throat. Winding my way back up through the ferns, the evening was thick with an all-encompassing dark. In the distance, I could see the smoke rising from the s'mores pit like smoke signals, and beyond that, the pinpricks of The Copperhead's windows, glowing feverishly against a black sky.

I imagined that Bob was wandering the halls, sloshed, while his mother retired to her room. Carla, meanwhile, would be drifting too. Probably wondering, like Bob, where my mother, the life of the party, had wandered off to . . .

I batted the branches away from my face and quickened my clip.

Looking back, so many of the grown men in my life felt invisible—and Dad, who was the most absent and in some ways the least approachable of all, ended up being the most alive of them, even now.

Without meaning to—with no clear idea of where I was heading, other than away from my mother, away from the water, and out of the woods—I walked straight into the curved trunk of the horseshoe tree my mother and I had stumbled upon the other day. Steadying myself against it, the bark felt warm and rough against my back. I could hear laughter from the fire pit and caught another waft of cooked marshmallow on the breeze. Was that Bob's voice I heard? Carla's hyena laughter?

When I eventually returned to our room, I expected my mother to be passed out in bed when I returned. What I came upon instead was a room flooded with light, the beds turned down, a mint chocolate and a towel puffed into a swan on our pillows. My mother, gone.

Chapter Thirty-one

I was as young as six, maybe seven, when my mother decided to drive up to her family's camp in Maine for a few days—"Just the two of us, Eva." She'd rushed me into the back seat. "Buckle up!" she beamed.

I can still remember my delight, not long after arriving, when our camp neighbors—a middle-aged couple that lived year-round on the other side of the forest—invited us for an afternoon on their pontoon boat. Accompanying them was their teenage son, a boy I can remember being mildly fascinated by—for he was neither a child, nor a man, but instead, all tanned, lanky arms. A blond mop of hair and the faintest peach fuzz at his chin.

The parts of the pontoon ride I remember: my mother joshing around with the couple over card games; canned beer for the adults and colas for the teenage boy and me; the woman offering me peanut butter sandwiches and coconut cookies; her husband and son taking a small rowboat out fishing. My mother waving to them from the hull. Later, from my perch behind the wheel—the woman showing me how to play Captain—my mother sat between the father and son, my mother's face turned up to the sky, coral mouth wide open in laughter.

The afternoon sponged on in the way that hot summer days on the ocean move. The pontoon sturdy on the water, which was calm. Silver cutting the blue from the sun.

At one point, the woman showed me a magazine, *Highlights,* which I recognized from the library. By then, I was already a fast reader, but embarrassed by my abilities. I can remember being stung when I overheard Finn describing me as "smart as a whip" to his son. At the time, I hadn't known what the idiom meant and regarded it as an offense.

And so I skipped the magazine's storybook pages and turned to the "Hidden Pictures" activity at the back. I became quickly engrossed in it trying, with a feverish determination, to identify the objects in the illustration that didn't fit. I can still recall the one that stumped me. The drawing showed a giraffe giving a lion a haircut. The first object I found that was wrong was a bone, which was randomly placed alongside the barber giraffe's long-toothed comb. I'd found the slice of watermelon and the hammer, but where was the snake that was also supposed to be hidden somewhere in the picture?

I was so absorbed in my scrutiny, it must have taken me an extra beat to notice the couple fussing over me. For there was the woman, the back of her hand to my forehead; there was her husband, pressing me with a bottle of water.

"She doesn't look well," the woman said.

"Drink this," her husband pressed.

"Eva, sweetie?" The woman cupping my chin in her hand, her husband tucking the copy of *Highlights* under his arm. "I think you've had too much sun. Let's get you into the shade."

I craned my neck to look for my mother, who was playing cards at the table with the son, her foot brushing against his calf at the same moment she crowed. Tilting her head back like she always did before the husband joined her and she showed them her hand.

Back on shore, the woman tried to slather me in aloe vera, but my mother told her no, we had to go. Thanking her before taking me by the hand and dragging me back through the sand and up to our camp. She paused on the porch, considered her keyring, turned to me, and said, "How about a ride into town? It's still light out—no sense wasting a beautiful day inside. What do you say, sweetie?"

Town was packed with the summer crowd, the smell of the saltwater and the lap of the water hissing against the rocks. The lanterns lighting the docks.

My mother and I split a hot fudge sundae at The Sweet Sisters, and went to see Disney's *Beauty and the Beast* at the Carmike

Cinema. It was pitch dark by the time we got back to camp. My mother surprised me when she climbed into bed beside me—usually, she tucked me in and then went back downstairs to be with Dad. *But Dad isn't here,* I remembered all at once, because for a moment, I'd forgotten it was only the two of us who'd left for camp. Just like my mother had said.

At the time, I had never known my mother to leave me, so the aching abandonment I met when I woke in the middle of the night to discover my mother gone, the loft empty, was one that never quite left me.

I don't know what I was thinking when I wandered down the stairs, out the cabin door, and into the woods. I cannot say what happened between entering the trees and finding my mother. What I remember is the smell of the woods, the soft of the ground underfoot, the damp of mushrooms and wildflowers, moonlight a mosaic on the forest floor. When I found my mother, she wasn't alone. She was lying in the undergrowth with the teenage son from the boat.

Later: my mother swooping me into her arms; me, with my hair in snarls, my elbows and knees covered in mud. Me, shivering in the leaves, wearing only my thin nightgown, my skin blistered from sunburn. The boy from the boat waiting awkwardly at my mother's elbow as she carried me away without looking at him, without saying anything to him even after he offered to help.

This was a memory I'd long ago shelved, a memory I used to question. One I used to push down, telling myself, *That never happened.*

But, of course, it had.

Back down the elevator, I went about The Copperhead in search of my mother.

Huddled on the couch in the library, was Carla. Under the defiant gaze of the stuffed jackalope, Carla's widow's peak looked particularly severe. She drew her jumble of blankets to her neck.

"Have you seen my mother?" I asked her.

"Your mother?" she yawned.

"Leonora?" Bob stepped out from around a shelf. "Is she around?"

"Oh!" Carla hiccupped. "It's you!" She fluttered her eyes at Bob. "I thought it was just me in here. Me and the animals."

"Eve," Bob looked at me worriedly. "You can't find her?"

I stared at the empty glass Bob held at his side. "It's *Eva*," I said. "And no," I looked at him firmly. "I can't find her. But what about *your* mother, Bob? Can you find her?"

When I rang the bell at the front desk, the same receptionist from check-in came lumbering out from the back. She was tired, which meant her resemblance to a labradoodle was even stronger.

"I'd like to check out," I said, "for my mother. Her name is Leonora—"

"There she is!" sang my mother.

I whirled around on my heel to face her. Clad in one of the spa's puffy robes as she traipsed up to the desk, Leonora Marino was smashed. "*Loved* the whirlpool, Dot," she said to the receptionist. "Thanks for the suggestion! I never would've guessed it was twenty-four hours."

"Well, it isn't. But when my manager mentioned your aunt, we thought we'd—"

"Is it really time to go, Eva?" Leonora Marino smiled at me. "Too bad you didn't have time for a soak. I suppose we'd better have the boys fetch our bags—"

"You still have one more night." Dot was jiggling the mouse of her computer, waking up her screen. "It says we have you booked for—"

"Oh, but Dot," my mother looked at her sadly. "My aunt's just died, remember?"

"I'll drive." I held my hand out for the keys.

Chapter Thirty-two

Blackened and crumbly, the bungalow's dining room ceiling looked like a smooshed Oreo.

My mother and I were silent as we waded through the debris. I could feel the ash seeping into our skin, smelling up our hair and clothes. Miraculously, soggy chunks of the Peep cake, probably blown about from the power of the fireman's hose, still covered the floor.

It was amazing the fire didn't do more damage. The glass of the hanging mirror bubbled black at the center. Among the things we found relatively intact were a charred chair leg and a brass candle-holder; a patch of my whitewashed bellbottoms from the quilt my mother had made using my clothes.

My mother broke the silence. "I'm not sleeping in here."

"You don't have to. We have bedrooms."

"No. I mean in . . . what do you call it? The bungalow. I'm not staying in the bungalow," she paused. "I'm not tired, are you?"

"Okay, it's nearly dawn now. This isn't normal, it's nocturnal. You didn't sleep at all on the drive."

"Yeah."

"So . . ."

"So I'm going outside."

"Mom, there are plenty of rooms."

"Well I want to get out of here. I'm going to the beach."

I followed my mother up the stairs. She paused on the third-floor landing, in front of the window where Sebastian and I had first seen her and Finn kissing.

Something about the glass of the windowpanes gave the illusion of rain. Even when the sun was sharp and shining, you'd peer out the dappled glass and think the sun was water.

My mother began pulling blankets and sheets from the linen closet. Slung her finest goose down coverlet—a Kaminski family heirloom, embroidered in roses—over her shoulder.

"C'mon, Mom. Stop it."

My mother dragged out a stepstool, strained to reach the uppermost shelves. A big blue tarp cascaded to the floor. "No, honey. I just don't want to be in a house that smells like smoke. I'd rather be by the water. Call me a bear, but I'm just following my instincts. I want to go to the beach." Heading back for the stairs, my mother added, "I'm taking a leaf from your book and hiding from the world, darling."

A sandal weighing down either side of the tarp spread out beneath her, my mother sat down by the water, the embroidered rose coverlet bunched up around her.

When I saw her shoulders heaving, I thought she was laughing. Which was what my mother typically resorted to doing whenever discontent struck. But the second I touched her shoulder, I realized Leonora Marino was crying. Finding my mother like that broke my heart. Come what may, she was my mother and I loved her. I sat down beside her, looked out at the ribbon of orange on the horizon. It was nearly daybreak.

"Why does this keep happening?"

"What?"

My mother shook her head. "We keep running away."

"You're it," I tried to keep my voice light as I tapped her. Something inside of me shifting or colliding—I wasn't sure which. I was falling apart. I thought back to that book by Rushdie Brouhaha, which I'd discovered in Barnes and Noble back when the pumpkin spiced everything rolled into the café, and I ended up spending all my money on self-help books and soy lattes when I was convinced that even Shiloh couldn't help me. In *The Art of the Apology,* Rushdie Brouhaha advocates forgiving by means of offering gifts in the attitude of the Old Testament magi: put on your forgiveness shoes, grasshopper.

My mother forced a dry laugh. "Ted's due back today." She stood.

I walked the shore with her, told her how excited I was for her—"Your wedding is going to be beautiful, Mom. Really." I promised I would do whatever it took to make the wedding fit her vision and apologized for not helping more. "That was selfish of me."

I told my mother I would set things straight. "I'll set a thousand turtledoves free the moment Ted Turbine kisses his bride!"

"You don't need to do that." My mother lifted her hand. "You just need to show up."

It wasn't until I noticed how close we were to the surf—what had once been the sand beneath us now packed and wet—that I realized I'd followed my mother to the very spot of beach I'd avoided since last spring. Last spring, after I'd sprinted from the rocks I watched Sebastian jump from.

My breath ceased, taking it in. Back behind us was the bungalow and Finn and Sebastian's cottage that no one lived in. Between them lay the expanse of green turf I'd crossed to get to my mother and Finn. Had I glanced back at the waves, once green and enormous, to see them recede? Or had I even taken the grass, running instead in the street—that black tarmac that got so hot in the summers, it could bake the bottoms off your feet?

I couldn't remember.

But I did remember. Because I'd taken the latter. I'd left my sandals behind. Later, when feeling returned to me slowly, I found the bottoms of my feet cracked open.

I started when my mother grabbed hold of my hand.

There was the outline of a person rising out of the distant waves, the figure looming larger as it drifted toward us.

"Mom?" I pointed with my free hand.

As my mother squinted out at the surf, I thought I could hear her breath hiss.

"Eva . . . ?"

I closed my eyes, opened them. The figure was still there, shrouded in a glimmer of silver-green light. I let go of my mother's hand. Took a step closer, and then another, until I stood ankle-deep in the water.

"Do you think I should go through with it?" My mother's voice trailed off with the wind.

Acknowledgements

I would like to thank Texas Review Press and Clay Reynolds, champions of the novella.

I am also grateful to the Department of English and MFA Creative Writing Program at the University of Alabama: My appreciation extends to the faculty and students for their example, support, and sheer good spirit. Special thanks to the University of Alabama Alumni Association for its generous License Tag Fellowship, which afforded me an academic year's worth of time and support to immerse myself in my work.

I am enormously appreciative to my family and friends for their unwavering support. To my teachers and friends: Robin Behn, Joel Brouwer, Angeline Chiu, Alexis Fisher, Michael Martone, Wendy Rawlings, and Kellie Wells.

Special thanks to Kim Davis, for her continual support; to Elizabeth Evans and Savannah Burns, for their editorial work; to Nancy Parsons, for the gorgeous cover art.

Thank you to my loving and inspiring grandparents, Yetta and Theodore Ziolkowski; to my deliciously comical and kind aunt, Alice Faye; and to my heroic "papa," Dave Houston.

Thank you to my adoring and big-hearted in-laws, Linda and Fred Bishop, who have offered me every kindness in the world.

I write in memory of my grandfather Charles; my aunt Lana; my "mima," Jan Houston, and my dazzling grandmother Rose.

Thank you to my sister, CeCe—stalwart painter, sculptor, and friend.

Thank you especially to my husband, Daniel Bishop, for his infinite faith in me and my work, and for his enduring sense of adventure—you fill me with such happiness, Dan.

This book is dedicated to my parents, Lee and Eric—writers and scholars, your brilliance and dedication to your work never ceases to inspire me. Thank you for your astonishing encouragement, for all the opportunities you've given me, and for providing me with a childhood filled with books. My gratitude and admiration are boundless.

CPSIA information can be obtained
at www.ICGtesting.com
Printed in the USA
LVOW03s2334060218
565545LV00001B/7/P